Marcia Ph...
The case of the busybody landlord

That Ed Hollingsworth sure is nosy! And he seems to have an opinion on everything. For instance, my taste in paint, my choice of friends, even what I should wear! It wouldn't bother me so much if he weren't so darned cute.

The more I yell at him, the more intrigued he gets. And that's bad news. Because the truth is, I do have a secret. If Ed gets much closer, I'm afraid he'll figure out what it is. And then we'll both be in *major* trouble. So I'll just have to find a way to resist the infuriating blond-haired hunk....

Dear Reader,

Here I am, your new correspondent. I admit to having been a little nervous as to what I might say in this letter, but then I started thinking about this month's books, and Lass Small's *The Case of the Lady in Apartment 308* got me thinking. What it specifically got me thinking about was my own house, which I own. Well, okay, the bank and I own it—and I bet you can guess whose is the larger share. Anyway, the thing is, I've started to think it might be nice to rent, not own. That thought first occurred to me after I fell down the stairs with the lawn mower. (Don't ask.) Then there was the night—early morning, really: 2:00 a.m.—I nearly electrocuted myself trying to turn off the attic fan. (Don't ask about *that*, either.) And then I read about Ed Hollingsworth, and now I'm sure of it: If I can have a landlord *just like him*, I'm putting my house on the market and renting from here on out!

After you finish falling in love with Ed, check out Celeste Hamilton's *When Mac Met Hailey*. It's equally delightful, the story of a man looking for…what? A wife? A mother for his daughter? Or just a hot date? Whichever it is, he finds her in Hailey Porter. Don't miss it.

See you next month—hopefully with no more housing traumas to report. Until then, enjoy!

Leslie Wainger
Senior Editor and Editorial Coordinator

Please address questions and book requests to:
Silhouette Reader Service
U.S.: 3010 Walden Ave., P.O. Box 1325, Buffalo, NY 14269
Canadian: P.O. Box 609, Fort Erie, Ont. L2A 5X3

LASS SMALL

The Case of the Lady in Apartment 308

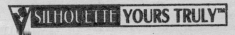

Published by Silhouette Books
America's Publisher of Contemporary Romance

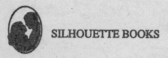 SILHOUETTE BOOKS

ISBN 0-373-52023-9

THE CASE OF THE LADY IN APARTMENT 308

Printed in U.S.A.

Dear Reader,

How strange to find ourselves moved from Fort Wayne to Indianapolis! Next to San Antonio, TEXAS, we found Fort Wayne to be one of the best cities in all of the United States, and not one of our kids stayed there! How rude of them. So now we have moved to Indy.

It is the size of my San Antonio, and it is amazing to be in a busy big city again. It takes a little readjusting, the learning of streets, which stores, how to get there, that sort of thing. But it is stimulating.

It's a hundred miles closer to San Antonio. Of course, after all these years I've adjusted to living away from home. Well, almost. I wonder how many of you all have been uprooted and moved to another place. It seems as if the whole country moves around. But there are people who stay put. I bow to those rooted ones, and I salute the adventurers...like those in this story.

With my love,

Lass

Box 30012
Carrollton St. Broadripple
Indianapolis, IN 46230-0012

To
Margaret Gosselin
who grew up in Peoria
and to
Bill Small
who "observed" Peoria gambling

1

The first of July in Peoria, Illinois, the weather was hot and dry. One of the citizens was thirty-seven-year-old Edgar Hollingsworth, who was well-made and tall enough. His hair was a light blond and his eyes were a surprisingly dark brown. His hair and eyes were an interesting combination, which women adored.

On the day in question, Ed climbed the newly mended stairs to the third floor of his apartment building. He carried a self-composed eviction sign to tape on the door of 308. Occupying that apartment was a recalcitrant, nonpaying woman who received government payments, plus.

Ed was disgruntled.

He'd inherited the renter when he bought the building. There had been no recorded payments since Elinor had paid double to get into the apartment. The rule was a month's rent down plus another month's rent in case the renter took off in the middle of an unpaid month.

That second payment was supposed to be a security payment. It was explained on the book that the "old woman" would get it, in "a couple of weeks" or soon. There was no notation that she ever had.

The next rule was payments could be only three days late, then a late fee would be added. Under very rare circumstances, if it was necessary, the owner could give the renter a month to pay up.

By then, Elinor had already had five months' free housing.

Well, Edgar was new to the business of renting, and he'd still had a susceptible heart. That heart was hardening.

Elinor hadn't taken off; she just wouldn't pay. She never answered the door. The locks had been changed . . . by her.

Ed couldn't find the copies of those keys. If there was an emergency, the door would have to be broken down.

Ed hadn't seen hide nor hair of her in all that time. She was either very clever or seldom there, for he'd not been able to contact her.

His unanswered reminders had finally been delivered by certified mail. There had been signed acceptances by a variety of signatures. That's how Ed had found out she had two men living with her.

Two men? At her age? Well, maybe they'd just been indigent friends.

At thirty-seven, Ed was still a young man and he thought "old" people were beyond such exercises.

Ed's basic problem was that he was an honest man with a tender heart. He didn't harbor even one Simon Legree gene.

He found it quite difficult to accept that honesty could be a problem. So after three notices of rent overdue, he was going to threaten to evict his recalcitrant tenant who, by this point, had not paid rent in an accumulated nine months. Ed ought to just padlock the door. But, being new at the renting business, he couldn't yet do that to an old woman.

That day, Ed got to the apartment and hesitated about putting tape on the recently refurbished door. He paused to consider the door. It was a good one. He'd done a lot of work on the place even before he was eased out of his middle management job in a local manufacturing company.

He'd been one of the few who had seen that his release was inevitable. The company was top-heavy with salaried men...and a few women. It was the men who were let go first.

Letting the men go made the company seem gentle toward women. That looked good, but the reality was that the male salaries were higher.

Despite reassurances that the cuts had already been made, Ed had understood he would eventually be one of those encouraged to leave, to explore new horizons.

The knowledge had hit Ed when the company released his good friend Mark, a valuable man. Mark had made more than Ed. Ed knew that in the release of the next bunch, Edgar Hollingsworth would be tapped. He wasn't married. His departure from the company was inevitable.

Having witnessed the discards' frantic scramble for other jobs, Ed knew it would take some doing before he could relocate . . . if he ever could. Even before his job was terminated, he had researched what he should do.

To get some workable cash, he had sold his dream car to a friend who'd envied him, and the price was right for both of them. To replace the car, Ed bought a station wagon that was solid, reliable and unnoticeable. It was brown.

He sold his condo with some pangs, and just after that, he bought two rental properties.

The compound's scalloped and spiked, iron fence surrounded the languishing complex with a rusted iron bar gate, which opened onto the cracked, concrete apron of the wide driveway. A great oak's spreading branches dominated the center of the courtyard. It was elegant.

In that complex was a painterly-painter. One who was wonderfully talented. Added were his wife and their strangely unique nubile offspring. There was an older couple who'd lived there since they'd retired on a pension that was smaller than they'd anticipated. There were three bachelors who invited the whole complex to their parties so that no one could complain about the noise. And there was the now-jobless Edgar Hollingsworth.

The elegant compound had been built with care long ago. The apartments were connected around a stone-block paved courtyard. It was probably a white elephant and no good for anything. Ed had never seen anything so eye-filling. However, the twenties' complex was elegantly unique. The view upriver was soothingly wonderful.

He'd chosen one of those apartments as his.

Before the stock market crash of the late twenties, in a time of artistic adventure, was when the sprawled, one-story complex had been built. There was every indication the riverside bluff area would be built up with posh homes.

That was delayed, first by the Depression, then World War II. The building of the area's houses didn't happen until after that war. The bluff project had developed into 1940's postwar, box houses.

And since then, in the proliferation of houses around it, the predictable individualism of people had emerged. The houses had slowly been expanded and altered from the original boxes. Trees had been planted and the greenery had proliferated

It had become an attractive area.

Ed Hollingsworth's other purchase was the four-story apartment house. It had a sturdy brick facade and a rather borderline mess inside. It was less than a mile away from the elegant compound. And there were undoubtedly shortcuts Ed could discover.

The apartment building was in an area that was neatly staunch. It was convenient to the surrounding area's shopping and not far from the Illinois River. The brick building was worth the effort to smooth it out and tidy it up, after it had been reroofed.

Ed had paid to have the more complicated and needy roof repaired and the roofing replaced. That was a tough job. With his office's downsizing, Ed was doing the renovation—since he now had so much free time.

Ed's pragmatic father had taught his sons to fix things. With that background, Ed also had the energetically helpful branch library which could find how-to books from all over the country. Ed's talent, for salvaging and rebuilding, was being expanded.

Ed's primary problem was that he'd had too much fun as a bachelor. He was thirty-seven and still not married. He continued his contact with a wide expanse of friends, who worked days. However, he'd noticed that the single women weren't crowding him with smiles and rubbings.

He was no longer financially alluring.

At the deadbeat Elinor's apartment, the reluctant Ed began to press the cardboard notice against the door. The latch clicked softly and the door slowly opened.

The woman inside was surrounded by various scattered items. She was packing to sneak out? Was *this* Elinor? How surprising!

Ed stared and his lips parted. He looked very vulnerable.

The woman turned and glanced over her shoulder, somewhat disgruntled. Seeing the tall man looking so rivetingly at her, she gasped.

Ed had never laid eyes on Elinor. He'd been missing all—this—all this time? Had he seen her before then, he'd have been willing to pay her rent for her! And she'd already had two men living with her? No wonder.

He handed her the eviction notice in an automatic, nonnoticing manner.

She read it and handed it back. "You have the wrong apartment."

In great surprise, Ed shook his head to deny being wrong as he asked, "Aren't you Elinor?"

"No. Who are you!" She was positive and alert.

He backed out the door somewhat, in order to lessen the threat of himself. He asked, "Where's Elinor?"

Standing straight, the woman shrugged as she watched Ed with some sober regard.

"I'm the rent collector, and Elinor is four months past her limit. Is she living here? Have *you* been living here? If you're not Elinor, who are you?"

The mesmerizing woman again shrugged, but in a normal way that was absolutely fascinating. She re plied, "I'm Marcia Phillips. I've paid two months' rent."

"Let me guess. You're subrenting from . . . Elinor Hopkins."

"Yes. She's paid ahead."

"She has been living here for at least nine months and apparently hasn't paid anything since the first month's rent. She's hornswoggled you for two months' rent."

The nubile woman looked at Ed. He saw as she first rejected, then gradually accepted that what he said was true. She frowned and considered him. Then she asked, "Was she . . . indigent?"

He avoided being entirely open and honest as he replied, "I've been handling the renovation of this building for four months. I'm responsible for collecting overdue rent and I've never laid eyes on her. She's as slippery as an eel. Apparently, she bilks everybody, every time. And now, she'd done it to you."

She guessed, "She was destitute?"

If the watching female was that softhearted, no wonder she'd been suckered in by Elinor. Ed explained with some impatience, "According to the house gossip, that woman sucked blood everywhere. She was on welfare. She got her clothes from Goodwill, she was a devoted user of the Salvation Army, and she had free meals from the Catholic church down the street. She was a clever, practiced deadbeat."

Then he added in amazed disbelief, "She had two men living with her . . . and she was probably charging them, too."

"They smoked the cigars."

He shook his head. "It was probably Elinor."

Marcia Phillips nodded with slow thoughtfulness.

"Unfortunately, she was also crooked."

"If she hasn't paid you in four months, you ought to have the money I gave her."

Now what was he supposed to do?

The fascinating woman appeared to droop slightly. She looked around and out the window and through the doors of the apartment. "I don't have any more money."

"It's not your fault." What a sucker he was. Elinor had probably moved out—after she'd told this nubile woman how to fool the new rent taker.

Ed had never told any of the residents that he owned either place. He didn't make that mistake now. He said, "I suppose you could work it out."

"How?"

"What kind of job do you have?"

"None. Not yet. I paint."

An artist? Great. His thought was sour. But as a painter, she really ought to be living up in the cheaper attic.

Disgruntled, he asked, "What do you paint?"

"Houses, barns, buildings, offices, whatever."

"No people?"

She looked at him over her cheekbones and retorted, "Not yet."

So she excelled in artistically depicting structures. She'd probably been in architecture but hadn't graduated.

He didn't need any paintings of anything. Especially not buildings. He'd never been drawn by drawings or paintings of structures. He leaned more to the pictures shown in *Playboy*. She could pose for that. She was really something.

She said, "Well, I guess I'd better pack up. Hope you can rent this place out. One good thing, I didn't even begin to clean it up."

That gave him an idea. "Are you any good at cleaning?"

"My mother taught Home Ec."

"That clean, uh?"

"Yep."

"You do anything besides painting? Or is your time comparatively free? I need somebody to clean up apartments. I'd pay you for that and we could forget one of the months' rent. Both months if you'll clean up this place, too ."

"I could, but you'd have to pay me enough to eat."

"Since you know I'm desperate, you have me over a barrel. We'll negotiate a deal."

She smiled.

Her smile was a whammy clean through his body. His breathing altered and his cells shivered. Moving with some care, he put the returned eviction sign down by the door. As he straightened, he put his hands into his pants pockets.

He told the ejected renter, ''There's another apartment down the hall that's just been renovated. You could bunk in there for now. Maybe you'd want that one more than this one. It's on the east so it's cool nights, and the sun wakes you in the morning.''

''I'll see.''

Her words made his hopes rise. She might not leave, after all.

He frowned at his thought. What difference did it make whether she lived in that building or not?

Well...

And he couldn't think of any argument to support his vibrating interest.

She asked, ''How many of the apartments are empty?''

He squinted, trying to decide whether or not he should lie. If she was going to live there and clean apartments, she'd find out anyway. He might just as well be honest. ''About half.''

''Do you advertise?''

''Not yet. The place is run-down and I'm beginning to get it shaped up.''

She guessed, '' Your dad a sailor?''

''How'd you know that?''

''Shape up. Shipshape.''

Ed grinned. ''He was like that with us kids. Being organized all of our lives, we're all doomed to be tidy.''

''What an irritation.'' She smiled.

"Well, I guess from what you say about your mom, you're probably a whole lot the way we are."

"Yep." She picked up a subtly elegant cloth Vera Bradley suitcase. "Which way?"

He grinned. "You're gonna stay?"

"I'll clean until I'm paid up. Then I'll paint for cash."

That wobbled him. He didn't *want* any paintings. But then as they walked down the bare hallway, he figured he could buy some of her paintings and put them on the hall walls. He wouldn't have to look at them. He'd do that.

He said, "Clean first."

"Yes, sir."

"Good attitude. Keep it." He used his master key on the apartment down the hall. Since the apartment wasn't Elinor's, he opened the door and stood aside as she entered. The apartment was furnished.

Ed looked at it with clear eyes. "It's a little stolid."

"Drab." She was turning her head. "The walls should be a light yellow."

He looked at the walls. She was right. "If...when you move back into the other apartment, I'll paint this one yellow for you."

"I can paint it."

He thought she would find it an interesting object to paint. She would label it something like Abandoned Room or No Home To Go To or something like that. It was depressing when he thought of living in the drab place day after day.

Having it cleaned wouldn't make it livable. He'd have to take another look at the other empty apartments. Maybe paint was what they really needed. The rooms were neat and tidy—shipshape—but they were drab.

He looked at the brown-haired woman with her blue, blue eyes. And he looked at her soft, blue printed suitcase of quilted cloth. She was a lady.

What was a fragile lady doing in a drab apartment building in Peoria, Illinois? He asked, "Where do you live?"

"Here?"

He smiled. But his husky voice went on and asked, "Where were you brought up?"

"Here." She shrugged.

He leaned back his head to nod one slow, serious time and said, "A real native?"

"Yep."

"I was an incident on a trip and I was born in Petersburg, Illinois, the heart of the Lincoln country."

"A Republican." She said that rather flatly.

"Yep." He echoed her own method of agreeing. "You'll learn."

His grin came slowly and his dark brown eyes sparkled unduly. "Teach me."

"I would doubt there is anything left for you to learn."

He sobered. "I'm not that old."

"You're that positive. You don't need directions."

"Guide me."

She put back her head and laughed aloud. It was a scoffing laugh, not an alluring one. She was not trying to lure him. How rude of her.

He didn't want to be lured. He wasn't in any position to take on a woman permanently.

He said, "I'll help you bring your things down here. You can have this key. I'll trade it for Elinor's keys."

"I hope she's okay."

"She's like an old cat. She's already landed on her feet. She's probably in another apartment and has already changed the locks."

"She did that?"

"She did."

Marcia held out her hand. "Give me all the keys to this place."

Even as he took them off his ring, he was saying, "I don't snoop. And I never did change the locks back on Elinor's place. Any other rent collector would have. I wasn't smart enough. I thought she was indigent until I realized she had two men living with her."

"Her sons?"

"I would seriously doubt it."

"Why do you say that?"

"She smoked cigars."

Marcia frowned as she considered. "Does that mean that cigar smoking men aren't fathers?"

"I would never have thought you were the picky type. You seemed pliant and kind."

"It's all facade."

He smiled as he looked down her body. "There's nothing wrong with—"

But she'd already caught herself and said, "I'll need paper to line the drawers. Are there any roaches?"

He put his hand to his chest in such a way that his elementary school play director would have gasped in admiration. He exclaimed, "Roaches? Here?"

She gave him a sideways look from disbelieving eyes and retorted with some sarcasm, "I'll keep track."

"You're the type that drives own—rent collectors crazy. I'd bet you get up in the night and sneak into the kitchen and turn on the light—just to check."

"Yes." She dismissed him.

She went into the bedroom and inspected the clean mattress as she set her Vera Bradley bag on its expanse. She tested the empty dresser drawers, the bathroom and, finally, the kitchen.

Since the kitchen was the last place of note, Ed figured she wasn't any kind of a cook.

What difference did that make?

None.

Being a man of his word, Ed helped her carry the rest of her bags to the other apartment.

As they were gathering up the last of her things from Elinor's place, she asked, "What colors are you planning for this apartment?"

"Green? Blue?"

"White."

His face held a distasteful look. "White?" He scrunched up his mouth as if he'd bitten into a sour grape.

She added. "The woodwork, too."

He looked at the worn carpet. It was gray.

On cue, she said, "It needs to be red."

He flinched just the slightest, uncontrolled wince. He repeated the word flatly, "Red."

She took her much smaller bundle and left the dull apartment. Her leaving made it duller, and Ed followed her out into the hall, closing the door.

He told her, "There are stores along Blake Street down the block. One sells work gloves."

"I saw it."

She was really kind of snotty.

She had no other comment to make. They walked in silence to her temp apartment. At her door, she put her things inside, turned back, took his burden and said, "Thank you." Then she disappeared inside her den and closed the door.

He heard the bolt slide into place.

He was barred from entering.

Well, he didn't *want* to enter her place.

It wasn't hers. She hadn't paid any rent.

What was he doing encouraging a female to take over a whole apartment when she hadn't even made a down payment? Well, she had. It was just that she'd *said* she'd made a double down payment on a "paid up" apartment.

That Elinor had some real questions to answer as to her conduct.

He really didn't think Elinor would understand anything about proper conduct.

Well, then, what about Marcia Phillips? Of what sort of conduct was she capable?

Why would he want to know? And just what sort of *mis*conduct did he have in mind? She'd given no signals, at all, that she'd be interested in any co-conduct with him.

Co-conduct wasn't a real expression. Co-horts was a word, and co-respondents, and then there was co-habitation.

What would it be like to cohabit with Marcia Phillips?

It was probably the recent indifference of the females he'd known and considered that had led him to speculate on this little wren who had landed in his cage.

It wasn't a cage; it was an apartment building.

He couldn't consider anything with any woman while in his unemployed circumstances.

Ed did the rest of his rounds in the four-story apartment building. He didn't check the third floor again. He did look down the hall as he went on down the stairs, but her door was closed.

She ought to keep it that way.

2

The rest of the day, Ed didn't hear one peep out of the intrusive woman. Not one. Ed had listened.

Marcia Phillips could have asked for cleaning equipment, or she could have inquired where what was in the neighborhood.

She could have wanted help in putting her things on top shelves. She could have thought of something if she'd wanted his attention. She hadn't asked for one single thing. He didn't see her again for the rest of the day.

What had she had for supper?

It wasn't any of his business.

Ed tidied his tools in the apartment basement's locked stockroom. With the day done, he fiddled needlessly. He looked around and knew full well it was time to go home to the compound.

He smothered the need to go check on his new renter. Actually, she wasn't yet a renter, she was a freeloader.

Ed's mouth turned down. His eyes flinched to recall he'd committed to buying some of her paintings. She was probably one of those artists who splash, throw the paint or dribble it on great canvases . . . or wood . . . Or apartment floors.

Actually . . . how did Ed know whether or not she'd paid one cent to the wily Elinor?

If the woman knew Elinor, she might be kin to the woman and just as wily.

Marcia probably *was* kin to that deadbeat woman. She'd moved in—having been told by Elinor that the new rent collector was a pushover for anything Marcia could dream up.

No way. Nuh-uh. Not Edgar Hollingsworth.

Somehow Ed was home, back at the rusty iron-fenced compound. Not remembering any of his walk, he looked around at the shadows cast by the setting sun. It was a beautiful place.

The great, protecting oak was a wonderful tree only about two hundred years old. That was young for an oak tree. Its branches stretched out and the lacy shadows were eye-catching as they splotched the stepped and deliberately askew concrete string of buildings.

Ed thought the woman architect who'd planned that compound had been a genius, far ahead of her time. But what pleasure it must have given her to have seen it built.

The fact that he could realize the visual pleasure of such genius would make him too critical of Marcia's artistic efforts. Ed's back muscles shivered to think of what all awful stuff the woman could concoct.

In the compound, there were fifteen separate abodes. None of the entrances was in sight of the next one. All had windows overlooking the river. That had taken skillful planning.

Since each unit had a basement, it had been easy to individually install furnaces which carried air-conditioning in the string of double-walled, connected houses. His remarkable buy sometimes tapped on Ed's conscience. No one had wanted it.

Even the lawyer who arranged the buy for Ed was envious.

"How could that jewel go unnoticed? Back in the grove of trees that way, no one paid it any attention."

Ed had.

Ed and his brothers had been Eagle Scouts, and they always looked at everything. There had been times when Ed had envied the freedom of other guys, but he did recognize the training his dad had given him.

His father knew how to take care of things. He taught that to his children. Because of his dad's training, Ed had a wider view of living. And he knew how to handle just about anything.

Well, not that new renter. She could be a problem. What if she just roosted there the way Elinor had? What would he do then?

He'd coerce his mother into routing her out.

What a cowardly thing to think about. His mother was mush with girls. She only routed males. Ed could handle males. He'd had enough practice in that from his older brother.

Once he was complaining to his parents about an aggressive fellow student who taunted and sneered at their second son. Even before he was finished, his mother said impatiently, "Ignore him!"

His dad hadn't said anything at the time, but later he'd gotten the boys together, along with two of the neighbor boys, and he said, "Ed's got a problem. Help him solve it."

They'd done it by tagging along with Edgar and crowding the several males who'd been crowding him. After that time, Edgar grew in height and muscle, and there was no longer any problem.

The muscle came from all the things the brothers had to do at home. Their dad cheerfully worked their socks off. They never had any idle time that Ed could remember.

Their mother taught them to cook. Since they all liked to eat, they endured the cooking. Gradually, they became quite skilled.

Edgar would respond to his mother's complaints about him still being single, "But you taught me to cook! Isn't that why men marry? To get somebody to cook for them?"

And his mother would complain to his father in disgust, "He's your son. Do something about this!"

His father would reply, "He's still young and tender. Let him harden up a little. He needs a little shine."

His dad hadn't made that reply lately. Just last week his dad had said, "Well, he's only two years older than I was when you trapped me."

And his mother had turned and lifted her nose at her husband. "I was engaged to another man."

"I'd told you all along that he wasn't suitable for you. You'd have led him by the nose and become so spoiled that no one could have tolerated you!"

She'd smiled in a smug way. "That's what you say, *now.*"

His dad lifted his gray eyebrows. "I was young and green. I didn't know I could lure a woman away from such a good catch. You surprised me."

His mother laughed in a throaty manner that Ed hadn't known mothers could use with husbands.

Ed stood there by the rusted gate and watched the approach of one of the tenants. He was older than Ed's parents. His name was Rudolf Smith and his nose was red.

Rudolf had lived in the compound so long that he could tell Ed where everything was threaded or hidden. On those kinds of communication, he told it . . . endlessly.

Rudolf asked, "Something wrong? Nobody's mad at you, you can come on inside."

And Ed replied kindly, "I'm just enjoying the leaf shadows on the white cement of the place."

Rudolf looked around. "It's pretty."

"Any problems?" Ed enquired.

"Nope. Just watched you standing out here like you'd sold the place and were taking one last look."

Ed laughed enough. The old man was very blunt. His sour comment was a high compliment because it said Rudolf liked the shadows cast on the compound just the same way Ed did. Rudolf wasn't a casual chatterer.

It had been Rudolf who said Ed ought to up the rent in the compound. Coming from that parsimonious man, the advice had been a sobering surprise.

Most of the residents had been there a long, long time.

Ed had called a compound meeting to hear any protests, but they'd all agreed. Only one couple was grudging, and they had the best income.

Rudolf had risen and growled, "With all the repairs Ed's made, we owe him."

Since it was Rudolf saying that, the raise in rents passed by a full, somewhat reluctant vote. They'd really had it easy for a long time.

It had been unexpected in Edgar's scheduling, So he took Rudolf over to the apartment house and had him look around and tell Ed what he thought about the setup and rentals.

Very seriously, Rudolf had advised, "Get it slicked up a little. It's really dead boring. When you've spruced it up, it'll look better and you'll get more renters.''

So Ed hired Rudolf for piecework and advice.

Rudolf loved it. He carried home all the tidbits of gossip to his wife. It had been a long time since he'd had a separate life from her, and they both enjoyed the stimulation of the gossip.

That evening, when Rudolf agreed the shadows were nice on the cement at the compound, he also said, ''Amy says to come by for your supper. She made too much again.''

That was always their excuse to share a meal with Ed.

Several times, Ed had noticed that Amy had had to add a can of sweet potatoes or slices of cheese to the meal because she hadn't expected company. She did that slyly and never turned a hair.

There are just people in this world who are interesting and very precious. And Ed's return meals to the Smiths were really very well done. Besides a mother's basics, a man of thirty-seven has had time to accrue talents.

Near the apartment house was the store strip Ed had mentioned to Marcia. While there were dress shops, the strip was made up mainly of old, surviving neighborhood businesses. There was a Laundromat, a select ma-and-pa grocery, a videotape rental, an elegant flower shop and a drugstore where stamps were sold and there was a postal pickup.

Beside the bank, there was the small library branch that Ed was using so well. They could find any book needed even if they had to send clear across the country to another library to find it.

The people who lived around there flocked to The Strip, as it was called by then, and they all visited and knew one another. They even smiled and said hello to strangers.

It wasn't a unique place. Such strips were all over the country. It was what had helped the residential area to survive. That and the river being so close by. While the houses might not be top-drawer posh, they were upper level preserved. And the whole area was convenient.

There were a lot of people living around there who had boats docked at a pier about six blocks down from the compound. Even Rudolf had a boat. Predictably, it was a putt-putt. No wild, roaring speedboat for Rudolf.

It was two days before Ed got up the courage to go deliberately to see how the new parasite was doing in his building. He climbed easily to the third floor and started down the empty hall—and the door to Elinor's old apartment was open.

Curious, cautious, he went over and pushed the door wider. There was a painter squatted down, painting the bottom of the wall. The whole floor was covered with canvas.

He was painting the walls . . . white.

White!

Ed cleared his throat and opened his mouth to give a marine sergeant's roar, when she turned her face to him. It was a she. Such fragile features were under a billed, paint-splattered, rigid cap.

She wore big glasses. She had no makeup on. But her coveralls were stiff with paint. She looked like a dribble painting by Jackson Pollock. He would have envied her splatters.

Ed bellowed rather loudly, "Who put you in here? What the *hell* are you doing, painting this . . . whi— Marcia? Is that you under all that paint?"

"Yes." She went back to painting.

Slowly the dawn broke in Ed's brain. "You're a *painter?*"

"Yes." She didn't glance around.

"I thought you meant pictures!"

"No."

"Now, just a minute." While he was speaking loudly, his voice tried to be reasonable. "You can't paint this room white. It'll look like a hospital."

"No."

He was stern. "I will not have this apartment painted a stark white!"

"I like it. I'll live here. I want it this color."

With some superiority, he assured her, "White isn't a color."

"To me, it's a background. I want it white."

He imparted wisdom: "Most renters want a cream color. It goes with anything."

"So's white."

He scowled at the painter who did walls and not canvases. "It's my apartment house."

"Oh?" She turned her head and gave him a paint-speckled glasses evaluation. "I thought you were the rent collector."

"I also rent out the apartments. If this is painted white, and you take off in the middle of some night, how am I to get this place rented again?"

She went back to painting. "There will undoubtedly be someone who is as discerning as I who will love having clean, white walls."

He repeated, "It looks like a hospital."

"It won't."

There is nothing more irritating to a man than a positive woman who doesn't agree with him.

How could a shorter, lesser-strengthened portion of humanity have the guts to counter him? Women are a God-given man's burden. Dealing with women is what cancels out men's sins.

Ed looked at the flaw in the universe that had lighted on his territory and thought. To hell with it

He turned and walked out of the room into the hallway and went on down the hall toward the stairs. It was only then that Ed realized he'd retreated.

No. He was giving her time to review her flaws and apologize.

He narrowed his eyes as he considered that a light green would look even better painted over that white wall. It would be okay.

Ed saw the white walls the next day. She was on a ladder—where did she get the ladder?

In some shock, he asked, "Where did you get the ladder? The last time I saw it, it was in the basement, locked in the toolroom."

"Rudolf freed it."

"He doesn't have the key."

She turned big, serious eyes to his—and it was rather overdone—as she said, "Do you suppose that Rudolf would pick a lock?"

"No."

She turned back to what she was doing and enlightened the creature by the door, "He did. I showed him how."

"You can pick *locks?*"

"Readily."

"So that's how you got in here that first day to paint."

She shrugged. "The key man wasn't here." She gave him a censoring look that identified him as the recalcitrant.

Her voice touched the words marvelously as she finished, "I dislike sitting, waiting and twiddling my thumbs."

He could understand that.

And as he was adjusting to her being logical, he realized she was hanging drapes! Orange ones. Orange! And only that one wall was painted.

He had the audacity to mention his surprise. His voice squinched up just like his face as he said, "Orange drapes with a white wall?"

Since it was obvious that was exactly what she was doing, she saw no need to comment in confirmation of his observation.

He questioned, "Corduroy? In summer?"

She instructed with some impatience, "You can't see through it."

He nodded in thoughtful, slow bobs.

Not even looking at him, she said, "Hold this."

He just went right on over and reached up easily and held the corner of the drape. And he got to watch her from another point of view.

She was, of course, standing on the ladder. She was stretched up, hooking the drapes into the holes on the rod.

It was an enticing and interesting view for a potent male. He swallowed but kept his eyes on her.

She said, "Let go."

He gasped at her insolence. He wasn't touching her!

She pulled on the material and looked down at him as she repeated, "Let go."

He did.

But she'd noted he was susceptible.

She licked her lips, looked away from him and went right on doing whatever it was she was doing to the drape in reference to the rod.

He put his hands into his trouser pockets and walked around a little.

She came down the ladder and lifted it easily out of the way. She then folded her arms and tilted her head a tad as she observed the hung drapes.

Ed was thinking, *She could look away from me!* He said to her, "They're noticeable." But his eyes looked down her body.

"My mother got a real deal on this material two years ago in the spring. My dad wouldn't have it in the house, so she split it between my sister and me. I love the color."

He ought to say something to support that but he squinted and just cleared his throat.

She soothed him, "When the pictures go up on the wall, it'll all balance."

Pictures? "We don't allow more than one nail hole per wall."

"I'll fill the holes with putty and paint them with a dab of... white, of course... and you'll never notice."

Obviously, there was more than one picture.

He turned his squint onto her and asked, "How many pictures do you intend hanging?"

"Well, I have friends who paint." She paused, "Pictures. Then there are the family pictures. I'm a godmother, and I have a niece."

She had said all that quite softly as one speaks to someone who is already grieving. What is it about men's rejection of nails in walls?

He accused her of smuggling. "I didn't see any pictures when you came in here."

"They're in the trunk of my car. Would you like to help me bring them up here? You don't appear to be occupied with anything, right now."

How could he refuse? Well, this would give him an opportunity to discard some of the pictures and leave them in the trunk of her car.

He made two trips, carrying the pictures. Two trips up two flights. She wasn't even breathing quicker.

Of course, she hadn't really replied to his long argument on leaving some of the pictures in the trunk of her car. She'd simply piled them on his arms and didn't really pay any attention to his succinct reasoning over excess pictures.

He took up pictures and held them against the wall. The frames were wood and heavy. She stood back and decided what should go where. Then she put those on the floor and arranged them to balance.

He got to pound in the nails. Every hammer stroke caused a flinch in his body. He did alter one nail. He *knew* it was over wires.

And he saw that she had a discreet pair of binoculars.

Hmmmm. A voyeur? He frowned over at the woman who was calmly doing whatever it was she was doing then.

She could be a bird-watcher.

He went over and put one hand between the drapes to peek out and see what she would see. The orange-colored windows overlooked The Strip.

That caused him to be very thoughtful. Deliveries? There were some posh stores down there.

Marcia was taking over *Elinor's* apartment. Were they in cahoots? Was Marcia to signal when one of the stores got a big delivery? The police were just lucky that Ed Hollingsworth was a good citizen.

How could he turn in the supple and intriguing Marcia Phillips? Hmmm. Intriguing Marcia Phillips. The first letters spelled IMP. Perhaps that was a sly indication of what she was?

Yep. The law was just lucky it had Ed Hollingsworth who was a good citizen.

And of course, that gave Ed a good excuse to see Marcia as often as he could. She tolerated him. She was kind. She worked the tail off him.

He had to admit the proliferation of pictures on her one painted wall was almost as fascinating as she.

She began to paint the next wall. Ed found she wouldn't work in any apartment on the other side of the building. She would paint any apartment he wanted that was on her side, including the two which looked down on The Strip, but she would not paint in the other two sides of the building.

Ed asked Marcia, "Why not?"

She regarded him with her lower lip pushed up in contemplation and replied, "The light."

"There's nothing wrong with our wiring. It's been completely rewired in the last six months."

"Daylight."

He considered her with a frown. And she returned his consideration with placid interest. Ed guessed, "Maybe you are an artist after all."

"After all?" She lifted her eyebrows.

"I thought you painted pictures."

She shook her head gently as she reminded him, "I have friends who do. They are having a joint showing down on the docks next week."

"Tell me when, and we'll go."

"We?" Her eyes had become riveted.

"You and I will go together so that I know if the artist is any good."

"Just look at the pictures."

He looked vulnerable. Men of thirty-seven can do that quite well. He told her seriously, "I have an older brother and three younger but I have never looked at any pictures except those in *Playboy*. How come you've never posed for any of the pictures?"

She gasped.

"I've looked at all the copies for the last five years and you're not in any of them."

She straightened in indignation.

He went right on. "I've noticed and you could qualify—easily. Hasn't anybody else said anything about pictures to you?"

She said a short, stopping, "No."

But he laughed. "You've got to be over twenty-five. You don't blush or wiggle. You're one of those new women who think—who consider they're equal to any man. So you paint to prove you can do it, just like any man can."

She discarded the conversation and went back to her dainty, precise painting.

She had no idea how many times he climbed those stairs to be sure she was all right. He kept track of every male who entered the building.

She never seemed to look up. She apparently didn't know he watched over her. She painted with the apartment door open. She'd placed a fan on the floor just inside the door. The windows were all open. Very little of the paint smell crept out into the hall.

He began to worry about her diet. He stood near her as she continued to paint and asked her, "What's your favorite food?"

"Peanut butter."

He realized she never gave him more than the initial, brief, identifying glance.

3

—**>** **<**—

Ed became concerned about Marcia's diet. While peanut butter was a good staple, she needed other nutritional input. Input? Yeah. She ate it.

But she needed more fruit and vegetables.

He went to his mother and said, "What are some good, easy, balanced meals that you can take somewhere and eat?"

His mother knew instantly he was interested in some female. At last. But obviously, she was not a cook. Hmmmm.

His mother asked with such an innocent face that appeared not too interested, but only casual and kind, "What sort of things does *he* like?"

Ed moved in the manner a man does when he sees a snake close by, but avoidable, and he said with a slow, casual hand opening, "'He' is me. I need some different foods to eat. Something I can carry with me."

He looked up with clear eyes to his radar mother and added in a gentle manner, "I'm out of work." He began that way as if she'd forgotten his firing. "I need to make pots of things and freeze them. I could take them out of the freezer as I need them. They'd be ready to eat when it was a mealtime.''

His radar mother's eyes narrowed slightly. Ed had explained too long and too much. It *was* a woman. He was interested enough to slyly feed that woman. Hmmmm.

His mother reluctantly rejected sauerkraut and wieners for a delicate woman. That had taken real backbone not to be lured into doing something so overly maternal. But she didn't know anything about this witch who was trying to lure—

Actually, it was her *son* who was trying to lure some indifferent woman?

How rude of the insolent witch!

The senior Mrs. Hollingsworth told her second of five sons quite casually, ''I have a loaf of my bread in the freezer. Your father sliced it a bit thick since he likes it that way—''

''I was hoping you had some of your rolls?''

''Well, yes, I do.''

''Then, some of those, and do you have any of your stew?''

''I . . . believe so.''

No voice could be as reluctant as hers in her replies.

Her sensitive, second son didn't notice.

His mother had recently assumed that—unlike his raucous, randy, older brother who already had five children—Ed would not marry. What the three younger boys did was their own choice, but she'd always considered Ed as her own child.

In the continuing effort of his acquaintances even she had touted several good, staunch, true women. But he'd never taken them out on a date singly. He'd had several other couples along, every time.

But he had dated singly. When he'd gone with the women of his choice, he'd never allowed anyone else along.

Ed was now thirty-seven years old and still unmarried. His observant mother had quite comfortably come into the idea that if his dad died before she did, Ed would move in and take care of her and the house...the yard, the errands. The grocery shopping...

It was something of a jolt for Mrs. Hollingsworth to find her son was probably thinking in another line entirely. Ed was concerned with some female's diet. That was very serious.

Ed wasn't aware of "serious." He was curious about the woman and feeding her was a way to observe her. She was a strange person. He couldn't figure her out.

In all of Ed's life, there hadn't been too many women who didn't wiggle around for his observation. Marcia didn't wiggle. She looked at him as if she knew more than he did.

How rude of her.

She had the ears of a cat. He'd come to the open door of the apartment she was painting, and she'd be picking up her brush. She wasn't just dipping it into the paint, she was picking up the brush and then she dipped it.

Instead of interrupting her painting, he was interrupting something else. It was a good thing he was paying by the apartment instead of by the hour.

But what was distracting her? And there were those discreet binoculars. Was she a lookout?

Was she nosy? Was she watching some other man? For whom? For...what? Why?

And Ed figured Marcia was in some sort of trouble and needed a strong male to take care of her. Somebody like Ed Hollingsworth.

He said, "You're still in this room?"

She cast a brief, patient glance his way and replied, "I'm careful."

He thought she'd be a lot quicker if he stood around and watched her. She wouldn't need to wander around and hurry back to the painting when she heard him coming down the hall.

She didn't seem to act guilty when he caught her that way. She just didn't want any questions? What distracted her? Who?

Since he did pay her by the apartment and not the hour, why did he care?

Well, after all, he was a time and motion expert. Many and many a time, he'd gone and studied how people could do a job more efficiently.

This female painter needed more concentration. But then... He wasn't anxious for her to get through with the painting. Although it took a good deal of his time to keep check on her safety, he didn't even notice how much time it took for him to monitor her. His time and motion checking *her* didn't count.

The most intrusive part of his life was the constant meetings and telephone calls trying to find a place that would hire him. He was very marketable. But he was getting pickier and pickier about what jobs were being offered.

He'd turned down three positions since Marcia had begun working for him. His conscience touched on that briefly, but he didn't examine the illogic of the blue-eyed reason.

It wasn't the woman who'd influenced his choice, it was the apartments. He didn't want to leave town and leave the supervision of the apartments to a stranger.

Right.

He said to the aloof woman, "I'll bring your lunch today. Can you eat about twelve?"

She looked at him with a weighing sobriety. Then she said grudgingly, "Okay."

No surprise, no smile, just that reluctant "Okay." The woman had no idea how to treat a man. She needed lessons. For her own life, she needed to know how to handle a man. He could help her in learning such skills.

He smiled just a tad.

She gave him a glance that a woman would give to a spider.

She probably didn't know about black widow spiders who ate the male after they'd mated.

He considered her. He wouldn't mind being eaten by her. He smiled and licked his lips. But he was discreet.

He wasn't thinking of cannibalism.

He regarded her. All he could see was that paint-flecked hat and the too-big overalls that were stiff with paint splashes, streaks and smears. Did she ever wash them?

He lifted his nose a little and tested the air. Since the fan was behind him, he moved casually to the other, downwind side. She didn't stink. He smiled.

Then he licked his lips and bit down on his lower lip. He was testing to see if she bathed? Think of that! Just because her clothes were paint smeared didn't mean she didn't wash them. She just didn't soak them in turpentine first.

With her clothes paint splattered that way, she appeared to be a real pro. But the clothing was too big for her.

Now that was interesting. Was she deliberately in large clothing? Or was she wearing someone else's clothes? Ed found the immediate response to the question was that his body would love to have her inside his clothes.

How strange it was for him to be drawn to an indifferent woman. Why her?

It was probably because no woman had hustled him since he'd lost his job. He was lonely. He'd dated, he was in groups with a date, he didn't have any trouble finding a woman willing to go out with him. But they were no longer anxious to trap him.

Every single one asked first if he had another job...yet. It was getting to be a nuisance. And he considered that Marcia had never asked him if he was employed...

Of course. She thought he was...by the owner of the apartment house. She thought he had the job of being a rent collector.

He asked Marcia, "Would you like to eat over in your place? Or would you like to go down to the basement?"

"The basement."

"We could eat at the table in your apartment."

"The basement."

Ed left in time to go back and set out their lunch. He'd set the table in the basement.

Walking down the stairs, yet again, he thought: Why didn't she find another job? Then he considered his own position. He, too, was doing something other than what he had been doing. And he wondered if Marcia had been in middle management and was another released discard.

So they had lunch together. She came into the basement, sat down and began to eat. She hadn't wiggled or smiled or even greeted him.

He said, "Hello."

She looked up at him with some puzzlement "We just saw each other upstairs."

"Are you hungry?" He smiled his killer smile.

"It's noon." She discarded that as a conversation subject.

So he asked, "Did you read about the new congressional bill this morning?"

She didn't bother to look at him. "I'll see it in the evening paper."

Ed settled a little and smiled. "Well, they—"

"Don't spoil my reading about it."

"I just thought you might like to know."

"I will, tonight."

So they ate in silence. She blotted her lips with the paper napkin. She did that as if it was fine linen. She laid it casually beside her plate as she would a linen napkin. Then she said with courtesy, "Thank you. That was very nice."

With that, she got up and went off, out of the basement.

She had used him.

Actually, she'd been courteous and shared his lunch at his invitation. She just wasn't interested in him.

Ed's view of himself slumped.

However, two days later, he invited her again to eat with him in the basement. He had pork chops with rice, canned tomatoes and peas with the pork drippings enhanced with Worcestershire sauce, cooked onions and some water.

His mother had made the meal. She'd given him two pork chops for his lunch, but he had shared the food with Marcia.

She ate it with some savor. "This is clever."

And when she'd finished, she commented, "With an elegant name like Hollingsworth, how did your parents name you—Edgar?"

She didn't like his name. He said, "My friends call me Ed."

She spooned the lime sherbet silently.

He said, "I'm really a homeboy."

She responded, "Marriage doesn't interest me, at *all!*"

That was clear enough. Ed felt somewhat deflated. Why? He wasn't seriously interested. But he considered her silently sitting across from him. Her eyes were downcast as she slowly, silently relished the sherbet.

It came to him that, while she had been emphatic about marriage, she hadn't rejected an affair.

And she *had* had two meals with him.

He perked up a little. But she rose and said, "That was nice." And again she strode out of the basement, leaving the used dishes on the table.

Ed thought maybe he ought to find a more suitable place to feed her.

Where?

It was the evening after that when Rudolf and Amy Smith invited Ed to go fishing early, early the next morning. "We'll have breakfast on the boat. We'll get back here about eight that morning."

And before he realized what his tongue was doing, he asked, "May I invite someone along?"

Rudolf perked up, but his wife elbowed him, and it was she who said, "'Course."

So Ed drove back to the apartment house and went up to the third floor. What if she was out on a date? So he wasn't anticipating any reply to his knock.

However, Marcia came immediately to the door and looked up at him as if she had expected someone. No big smile, just surprise he wasn't someone else. Who?

She asked, "Yes?"

That was all the greeting she gave him. And he indicated he was willing to enter the apartment and visit, but she stood firmly in the door.

So he stood there crowding the partially open door and gave his invitation. "Two people I know have a boat on the river. And they've invited me to go along tomorrow morning about six. We'll have breakfast on board, and Amy is a good cook." That's how he told her another woman would be along. "We'll dock about eight. Would you like to come along?"

She didn't move. But she looked at him soberly. Then she said, "Okay."

She'd agreed! But she hadn't smiled or moved out of the blocking manner by the door. She said, "I'll be at the dock at a quarter of six?"

"I'll come by for you."

"Okay. I'll be by the front door."

"I'm so glad you want to go along. It'll be nice."

"Okay." She moved the door a little to indicate the conversation was finished.

Ed stepped back. "I'll see you in the morning at the front door."

"Yes." And she began to close the door.

He said, "I'll bring the poles and bait." He smiled as if she would think *he* was bait for her.

She made no reply but began to close her door. The contact was over.

Ed had looked. He couldn't see that anyone else was in her apartment, but the door hadn't been all the way open.

As Ed stepped back into the actual hall, her door closed altogether. She hadn't smiled or said thanks or even tried to appear friendly.

Ed went down the two flights of stairs and out to his car. He got into it and considered. She really wasn't eager about him. Why did he pursue her? He didn't know.

Was it the challenge?

Surely he wasn't the kind of man who just had to see if he could attract some reluctant woman. Was he guilty of such conduct? Yeah.

He realized he'd been doing such foolishness all his life. He'd been doing that ever since he realized girls were wonderfully different from boys.

He was deliberately trying to attract a woman who wasn't at all interested . . . almost not at all. She was going fishing with him. Yeah. With him and the

Smiths. With another couple in a small boat, what did she have to worry about?

Why did she bother at all? With her nothing company at two meals, and now a fishing trip, what was the threat that lured her?

And he knew. Just like that, it came to him!

She wasn't going to pay her rent! Yeah. That was it, exactly! When it came due, she wouldn't pay. She was one of those.

Disgruntled, he drove back to the compound. He parked his car and then walked over to see the Smiths. Ed said, "We'll be there."

Rudolf grinned widely. His eyes sparkled with his curiosity. But Ed wasn't about to give Rudolf or Amy any satisfying expansion on who Marcia Phillips was. They'd soon see for themselves...and be disappointed.

As Ed walked back to his own place, he thought how curious Rudolf would become when he saw how indifferent Marcia was to her companion. Then Rudolf would wonder why Ed had asked Marcia along.

The next morning, there Marcia was at the door. She got into the car as he stopped. He said, "Good morning."

She gave him an acknowledging glance but said nothing.

She didn't smile but just settled herself in the car. She had her own fishing pole. It was a take-apart, clever one. It was not a bamboo pole.

How had she known it was his car?

So Ed puzzled on that in the brief silence it took to reach the pier and park on beyond.

The eager Smiths were on the pier. Marcia *smiled* at them and even shook hands. She had good teeth. It was the first time he'd seen them. Bad teeth was one of the reasons he'd considered for her never smiling at him.

He watched her shaking hands with both of the Smiths. She'd never touched Ed.

He didn't feel that she was "with" him. He felt that she had just used him for transportation. To be someone's donkey transport was diminishing.

He became a courteous, but silent observer who was helpful. He carried the two food baskets Amy indicated. Marcia carried her own pole.

The boat had an awning over it, and the poles were thin and sturdy.

Ed gave a helping hand to both of the women to step into the boat.

Rudolf didn't do that sort of thing. He went to the engine and started it. He used it on low power.

They didn't go speeding down the river. They putted along. At that time of summer, it was already light. It was a soft light and it was so quiet. The city was not yet rumbling along.

Peoria is a city of over a hundred thousand. It straddles the Illinois River, which is at least two blocks wide, and goes down Illinois to finally empty into the

Mississippi just above St. Louis. St. Louis is on the west side of the Mississippi.

In the quieter side waters of the Illinois River, Rudolf putted their boat along north of the city.

There were fields and trees. And the air was sweet. The sun wasn't yet up. The day was still hushed. Then barges came along. Grain barges. People were already working.

Of course, that was so in the city. Maintenance people, postal people, restaurant people were already beginning their days.

And the group of four was fishing. They anchored on the edge of quicker water and tossed in the bait on their fishing lines. Three of them had the traditional bamboo poles. Marcia had the clever rod.

With some curiosity, Ed watched her assemble the sections and bait her own hook. She was an independent woman who was not interested in allowing a man to help her or cosset her.

She wasn't what he wanted.

Amy chatted quite a bit with Marcia, but the latter's replies were scant. Amy didn't seem to mind.

Amy caught the first fish. Rudolf got the next two. And Marcia got one. Ed never did catch one.

He wasn't competitive.

The others all...well, it was their hosts who comforted Ed by saying they'd share their catfish with him.

Marcia didn't offer any portion of her fish.

She readily helped Amy put out their breakfast. She did that as if it was second nature. She'd never offered to help Ed with a meal or clean up after one. She'd acted like a guest.

Of course, she'd been invited to be a guest.

Well, she was there with the Smiths, too. She was invited as a guest, but she hadn't hesitated to offer help and she'd helped.

Amy had a real breakfast of ham and scrambled eggs with fat homemade rolls oozing with icing. Totally fattening. Absolutely *great!*

On occasion, Ed would turn his head minimally and give the woman—who was his guest—a judging look.

Ed realized she was a difficult woman. To continue to include her in his life would be a big mistake. She would give a man nothing. She would use him. That was all.

So Ed discarded Marcia before they even went back to the dock.

However, having been raised by his mother and father, Ed did take the woman back to her apartment. He didn't walk inside with her. He stopped at the front steps and allowed her to get out without any help from him.

She exited the car with silken ease, sliding out with no trouble. She carried her own things plus the fish she'd caught and she closed the car door.

Ed left. He drove back to his compound. There he showered and went back to bed. He lay thoughtfully considering. And once more he gave up on the woman altogether.

When he wakened, there were three messages on his answering machine. He turned up the volume and listened to that woman, Marcia, who said in a normal voice, "You are invited to a fish dinner tonight at 6:00 p.m."

That was all. No comment on the outing. Just that he was invited.

The second was his mother, who said, "Some woman called and asked how you like fish cooked. Who was that?"

As he was listening to the tape, his mother called again. She asked, "Who was that female?"

And her second son replied, "I don't know."

The third call was from a manufacturing firm out in California, which said, "We haven't been shaken off the continent as yet, and we're hiring. Your résumé was quite interesting." And the male voice added, "Please call John. I'm John."

The voice cheerfully gave the number and said, "We're looking forward to hearing from you."

Ed thought John sounded like a guy with humor and ease. Ed went to his file and looked up the company, what he'd read on them and what he'd written to them in application. It was a good company.

Maybe California was the answer to his restlessness. It was a long way away. Perhaps that's what Ed Hollingsworth needed.

When a man has abandoned an area—or a woman—his attitude changes. With the incident past, he can become hateful and critical... or he can be tolerant and kind.

He could be kind.

4

As Ed showered and shaved, he wondered how Marcia had found his mother's phone number. He hadn't dared mention the question to his mother. Her radar would perk up if Ed seemed curious about any woman.

Had Marcia asked Amy for the number when they were on the river? How would Amy have known? Did Amy know his parents' names and phone number? How? Why would she have given the number to Marcia?

When the two women had been talking, had Amy's ready talk been in reply to Marcia's questioning? Questioning about Edgar Hollingsworth?

Was...Marcia...curious about him?

He was going to her place for supper. She was going to share the fish she'd caught. They'd be alone together under different circumstances.

She'd tell him that her silence had been because she wanted his body so badly that she hadn't been able to think straight enough for idle conversation. That she hadn't dared to speak to him because she couldn't keep her hands off him.

Sure.

He'd go to her apartment with his bouquet of fl—

He was going to take *flowers* to her?

Well, that was ordinary. Most guys did that. It wouldn't be unheard of. He could pick some of those blue flowering weeds from in back of the apartments' garages. They'd be flowers, but nothing to knock her over.

It'd be subtle.

But she would be touched. She'd smile at him and say, "Okay."

And he'd pretend he didn't understand her submission. He'd give her his small, double whammy, subtle killer grin and say, "They're like your eyes."

She'd fold.

They'd quickly be naked and tussling around in the bed, with him trying his damnedest to keep up and—

The fish would burn in the oven.

He'd exclaim, "The fish!"

But she'd say... she'd say... "Who cares?"

She'd use his body recklessly with great lascivious hunger. She'd use her nakedness and busy fingers and hungry mouth to do outrageously sensual things to his helpless parts.

And when he finally lay, drained and exhausted, she'd say to him, "Move in here with me."

He'd gasp weakly and put up a protesting, defensive hand as he moaned in terror.

Ignoring his drained exhaustion, she'd just go at him again.

The water in the shower was cooling. He'd been standing there, daydreaming for too long. Well, she had invited him to supper. He'd go. He'd call her back.

Dressed and pacing, Ed went over the words he'd say in response to her invitation. He changed the words around. He added some compliments. He wrote it out.

He hadn't done that since he was sixteen! Twenty-one years ago!

But he did write it out. He switched words around and discarded some and added some and worked on the acceptance more than he'd ever worked on a résumé.

Women are a trial.

He tossed aside the written—and learned—acceptance when her answering machine replied. He said in a male voice that was his own, "Thank you for the invitation to share the catfish. I'll—" And the machine shut off.

There's no way to erase an answering machine. So Ed called back and finished. "—be there at five."

Why had he called her first? He still hadn't replied to John about the job out in California.

Well, taking a day or so to respond to a job interview wouldn't be unheard of. He couldn't appear desperate. A delay could work in his favor, making them anxious. He'd go over the material of the California office and figure out a neutral response.

Why would he waffle now when he'd already decided to go to California?

It was a move to contemplate quite soberly. After supper, he'd think about it.

Why wait until then? Was he going to give the silent, push-away woman of reality another chance?

No. He was just going to study the California option more closely

If he hadn't been sure about it, why had he applied?

Well... It was a long way out there. The ground wasn't steady, the trees burned readily and it cost more to live.

It wasn't cheap in Peoria.

But he owned two pieces of real estate which needed his attention.

Rudolf would love to take over the supervision of both places. And he'd do a good job of it. He was a fix-it man. That's why the compound hadn't dissolved entirely. And Rudolf hadn't even been hired for the maintenance. He'd just done it.

So.

Well...

Ed wanted another look at the woman. An aloof woman. She'd been frosty and withdrawn.

Yet, on her own, she'd invited him to her place. He wanted to see how she'd be.

That was more honest. Stupid, but more honest.

Why—stupid?

She hadn't given him any indication—at all—that she was even mildly interested in him. She'd never tried even to have a conversation with him. How could he expect *any*thing from such a woman?

She'd invited him to supper.

Big deal. He'd had her to lunch twice.

But not at his place. He'd served her in the basement on a wooden table.

The food had been good.

But women like atmosphere. They like elegance. They want to be pampered. Just watch. When she had him there for supper, she'd have the best linens on the table. She'd show off her culinary talents. It'd be a ball and a banquet.

Okay. So what was going on with her? She'd set him up. And he'd already discarded her. She'd flunked all the openings. Why now?

He'd know by—bedtime.

Dreamer.

It was an endless day. In the late morning, he did go over to the apartments. And he did go up the stairs to her apartment with an inner dither of anticipation.

Why was he there? What excuse could he give? He wasn't invited until five that evening. How could he begin?

He could offer to get anything she might need for supper.

Her door was closed and she didn't respond to his knock. She'd probably moved out overnight and her invitation was a touché of malice.

Disappointed, he took care of whatever needed to be done at the apartments, which wasn't much, and he went back to the compound. Then he went on a hike along the road down by the river.

Ed did nothing productive in that whole day. He was waiting for five o'clock to finally get there. Then he would see if she'd tricked him and had already left the place, or if she wanted to be friendly.

Actually he wondered if she would speak to him at all . . . if she was actually there.

How interesting that he considered her tricking him as plausible. If he felt that way about her, he ought to leave her be and have no contact with her at all. It was dumb to flirt with the knowing of such a woman.

But Ed waited for time to pass so that he could dress and go to her place. He felt as if he wasn't being very smart. He had trouble deciding what to wear.

He didn't wear a tie. But he wore good brown trousers and a contrasting cream sports jacket. His shirt was brown and so were his excellently shined shoes.

He was carefully shaven and his after-shave was so subtle that it would take a very friendly woman to even get a hint of it.

All of it was done with no idea that she would even be there. Or that she would actually accept him as a guest.

So he drove to the apartment house with no anticipation that he could actually acknowledge. His breathing was quicker only because he'd hurried.

Hurried? He'd been ready just about the entire day! He parked his car and locked it. But he did go behind the garage and pick a bunch for the blue weed bouquet as he'd planned. He considered it. It, too, would be a test. If she was actually still around.

Then he went into the very familiar building and up the worn carpeting on the stairs.

No one was anywhere around. There was a radio playing in an apartment on the second floor. He went on up to the third floor. No one was there, either, and the sounds were those of atmosphere. Nothing.

He went past the apartment she would have when she finished painting it, and went on to her temporary one.

That door, too, was still closed. He knocked discreetly, And he listened for footsteps. There was none.

But the door opened!

Had she been standing there, watching the clock, waiting?

She didn't smile. She looked up at him and said, "Hello."

She'd said hello!

He smiled and restrained the impulse to reply. His smile would do it all. He handed her the blue flowered weeds.

And she smiled! Her eyes sparkled. She didn't say anything. But she took them to the table and put them into her water glass.

The place mats were paper towels, the napkins were paper. The fish was ready to go into the skillet. The other skillet was covered and there was the fragrance of bread being baked...warmed?

And there was garlic. They were having toasted garlic bread. His mouth reacted with a rush of saliva. As early as it was to eat at five, he was ready.

Her brown hair was in a knot on top of her head and there were little stray curls by her ears and at the back. She wore no jewelry.

Who ever heard of a woman who didn't wear earrings?

He looked down her. She had on a white silk shirt with the sleeves rolled up, long black trousers, and black slippers.

She was out of that extralarge, paint-splattered coverall, and she was a lot skinnier than he'd remembered.

She was really well made. His hunger then was different. And he was still amazed that she hadn't stood him up.

She said, "This is the first time I've cooked a catfish."

He smiled. "It'll be fine."

"There isn't much damage I can do with the garlic bread."

He bit his lower lip to stop his laugh. She'd said several sentences to him. She hadn't talked that much to him since they'd first met.

She said, "I have to paint. But your supper will be ready in a minute."

He was stunned. He protested, "It's quitting time. You're supposed to sit with me and eat with me."

"I'm paying you back for taking me fishing." She could communicate. She knew words.

He was expansive. "You get half of the fish."

"I'm not hungry."

"If you make me eat alone, I'll go into a decline."

She tasted the word. "A . . . decline?"

"I have an uncle who lives in TEXAS and he says that whenever anybody crosses him. But he *can* go into a decline." He raised his eyebrows as he lowered his eyelids and he bragged, "So can I."

"How?"

He gave her his aloof glance and replied, "I slump and my face falls and I give up." He smiled and his eyes sparkled with his humor.

She said, "Bosh."

So he sighed deeply as he slid out of his cream jacket and hung it on one of the chrome-and-fake-leather chairs, which had seen better days. Then he unbuttoned his shirt cuffs and turned them back precisely.

He sat down and looked at her. "I'm ready to eat." And he put his hand to his forehead as if he was being very brave to endure.

When she made no response, his glance slid over to her and caught her bitten grin.

She said, "Where all have you taken your plays?"

"I'm not an actor, I'm just a simple man." Then he narrowed his eyes just a trifle and asked, "How do you make your living?"

She did an eye-catching shrug. "Painting."

He was kind. "You're really very good at it." But then his honesty kicked in and he added, "You tend to be slow and careful. When will you be finished with your apartment?"

"In about two days."

He frowned at her. "How can you live on what you make? You're so...careful that you're slow."

In her white silk blouse, her shrug was fascinatingly wonderful. His body tingled and he had to be careful his breaths didn't sound like an upset bull's.

Why her?

She was turned away, putting the fish into the hot skillet.

She put the waiting covered skillet onto the table and he peeked. It was cut-up potatoes, which had been browned as they'd cooked in grease. He smiled. To hell with cholesterol rejection.

He said, "Sit down. You don't get credit unless you share your company. I did. You have to reciprocate."

She sat down. "I didn't know rent collectors knew such a word."

His mouth just went right on and told her, "I've had a stickler for a mother."

She went to the small refrigerator and brought out a bowl of salad. It was well cut and had been tossed to distribute the dressing. There was lettuce, tomatoes and onions. Some croutons had been added. There were bits of green pepper. It was crisp and nice.

He smiled some more.

She watched the frying fish. She'd set the timer and it clicked along. When it dinged, she turned the fish carefully. And she reset the timer.

He wondered how she'd come to decide on how much cooking the fish needed?

She watched the timer, filled the glasses with water and put the warmed plates on the table. She took the covered skillet and removed the lid to allow him to take some fried potatoes.

Then the timer sounded, and she put the fried fish on a plate. She brought it to the table and said, "There."

He repeated, "You get half."

She considered. Then she sat down and cut the fish in half. She did that across the middle. He got the part with the head, she took the part with the tail.

How could a woman, who lived by such a big river, and had such a refined fishing pole, not know how to fillet a fish? There were probably other, more important things she didn't know. She had a few things to learn.

He reached for her plate as he told her, "Here. Let me fix that for you."

She said nothing but watched his face as he skillfully filleted the back half of the catfish. She didn't much care for fish.

He put the bones on his own plate and smiled at her kindly as he returned her plate. Then he began on his own fish, filleting it with dispatch.

She got up and found a soup bowl for him to use for the bones. And the fish's head. How gross.

They ate mostly in silence. He ventured several questions. "Did you go to school here?"

She replied, "No."

"Where?"

Vaguely, she said, "Over in Ohio."

He inquired, "What did you study?"

"Not painting."

He grinned and asked, "What?"

"General education. No particular skills," she lied.

"You do paint."

"My dad was a painter. I helped him."

"Most dads are tolerant of kids wanting to help." Ed was kind. "Did he teach you to be that careful?"

"He'd give me a whole wall. It was always in a closet or a back hall."

Soberly, Ed nodded and replied, "My dad did that, too."

"He also taught me to take apart the plumbing and clean it out. It took time."

Ed laughed. "My dad did that!"

Soberly, she communicated, "Being a father is a challenge. He does more interesting things than sweeping or dusting or washing dishes."

"I'd never thought of it that way."

She expanded the premise. "Men selected what domestic chores they'd do and allowed women to do the rest of it."

His humor brimming his eyes, Ed considered the rebel. "You couldn't change sex."

"I did try. Mother told me to kiss my elbow and I'd change." She added thoughtfully, "It's a wonder I didn't break my arm."

Ed considered her. "So you don't like being a woman?"

She turned her head slightly and gave him an amused glance along with that fascinating shrug and replied, "I grew into the role."

Without his permission, his flicking eyes were witnessing the result. "Yeah."

"Being female isn't easy." She shared that knowledge.

And he sighed. "Being male is worse."

She scoffed. "You guys have it so easy. Nobody harasses you, nobody crowds you. Nobody brushes against you. Nobody discards any advice or suggestions you give."

"You don't know the real world. Men have to run in packs. A lone male is chopped up. No matter what the circumstances, a guy needs backup. The worst possible scenario for a guy is . . . marriage. No. No. Listen. There, he's all alone, no male backup and has to handle *every*thing all by himself.''

She burst out laughing.

He laid his fork down and put his elbow on the table as he waited for her hilarity to abate. Then he said, ''Why, Marcia, whatever are you thinking about to laugh in that manner? Are you thinking about— gasp—*sex?*''

She bit her lip and watched him, her eyes spilling her laughter.

Earnestly, gently, he instructed the untried one, ''A man has to *train* a woman in marriage.'' He elaborated, ''What days he sleeps late, what sort of weather is fishing weather, who buys the beer for any gathering and what kind. Hush that. Who sleeps on which side of the bed. Who brings in the coffee and paper. A woman never realizes those are her chores.''

She tilted her head a little as she looked at him. ''You've never been married.''

''How'd you know that?''

''I believe Amy told me.''

''Almost all of my friends are married, and the guys spread the word. It sounds like such a strain, I've never been tempted to take the leap into the fiery pits of . . . the volcano.''

''You don't like the idea of being nailed down.''

''Men do that. Women submit.''

''Uh-oh.''

His face was so innocent and earnest, "They don't?"

"No."

"Well, I'll be darned! The guys I hear, tell it different. *They* say all those things. I've just not yet had the impulse to tackle a woman and train her."

"Train . . . her?"

"From what I hear, women come into a marriage thinking they're in control. It takes guys a tough lot of time just getting them settled. They don't even have time for friends right at first. The training takes so long and is so hard."

She scoffed.

"How many married couples have you seen out and about after they're married? They go on trips by themselves and they come home and lock the doors. A man has it hard." He shook his head and sighed. "You ought to just hear the tales they tell."

"What about kids?"

"What about them?"

"Does the dad take a hand in training them?"

"After the potty training and the food being poked into them and the bottles, then the dad gives them lessons in hamburgers and beer. They—"

"Beer!"

He was open and serious, "It's soothing to the screaming and yelling toddlers."

"Good heavens!"

He laughed so that he had to sit back and give the laugh room.

She watched him for a while. Then she accused, "You are a tease."

"I do try." He went back to the slivers of catfish he'd busily separated on his plate to make the meal last longer.

She considered him. "So you're not in the market for a wife."

"I'm not sure anymore. The guys I know who are married with little kids around, and some with high school kids, appear to be very contented.

"They include me in their activities, and they seem to be quite settled. It's scary. The guys I could always count on are talking kids' activities. They coach teams and drive kids and participate. I never thought it would come to this. What happened to all those good friends who were available anytime for anything?"

She replied readily enough, "They grew up."

"Are you married?"

"No."

He pushed. "Been married? Engaged?"

"Nope."

He tilted back his head. "Had any affairs?"

"None. I've been too busy."

He slid it in. "Painting?"

"I've done several things. Painting is another talent. I find it satisfying."

"I think you're wasting your brain."

"Since this is the first real exchange of conversation we've had, how can you judge me?"

He told her levelly, "I've watched you paint. Whose overalls are those?"

She smiled. "They're a keepsake of my dad's. The cap was his, too. I can tell you the history of each color."

And he wondered at her words.

He suggested, "I have some coveralls in the basement. Let's get the painting done tonight. It can air out—"

"Not tonight."

He took in a quick, surprised tiny gasp. "Why not?"

His reply had been different than she'd expected. She told him, "There's a friend sleeping in that apartment. He's just started working and needed a place tonight. I aired it all day. He'll be okay."

"You didn't tell me we had another occupant."

"The apartment wasn't occupied." She raised honest eyes to his. "I didn't think it would matter. It'll only be for a couple of days."

"You told me you had to paint tonight."

"I...I was giving you an out so that you could leave early."

"What made you think I would want to leave?"

"What makes you think I want you around?"

He could have indicated the table and her having fed him, but he simply looked at her. "Are you an honest woman?"

"Yes. But why would you believe me? You've already told me you don't much care for commitment."

"When'd I say that?"

"In telling me about your friends."

"Oh, well, sure, you see, yeah."

5

$\longrightarrow \longleftarrow$

Ed asked the woman whose name was Marcia, "Have you been married?"

"I've told you I haven't been married." Marcia glanced over at him and inquired, "If you didn't believe that, why would you assume that I'm not married now?"

"I don't think any man would allow a wife to paint alone, or live alone. He'd be helping you with the Elinor-accrued debt here, and he'd be helping you paint."

"What makes you decide that?"

"If you belonged to a husband or a bunch of painters, he, or they, would be here helping you out so that you could get back to the business."

"I'm independent."

He asked the ceiling first, "Who'd have the patience to wait for you to paint a house?" He looked at her sternly as he accused her. "You use that toothpick brush and you're too careful."

She retorted sassily, "I'm naturally neat and tidy. And I work by the job, not the hour."

"Those overalls are silent witness to how neat and tidy you are."

She laughed. She really did. She looked at him and her eyes twinkled with her humor. She told Ed, "I've been trying to discourage you so that you wouldn't be interested and distract me."

"Distract you...from *painting!*" He was totally unbelieving.

"Well, uh, yeah."

There was a knock on her door.

Marcia got up, and so did Ed. She went over and opened the door. "Yes?"

"I hear some guy in here with you?"

She opened the door a little more and gestured. "He's the rent collector."

Ed saw the big guy's glance go over him, dismiss him and then go on to stop on the table. Two places set. Obviously Ed was company invited there to eat.

The looming intruder said, "Okay." And he left.

Ed blinked. "Is he part of your painting crew?"

"On occasion, we work together."

"Painting?"

"He takes care of the bigger problems." She smiled at Ed.

"He could. What's his reach?"

"I don't know. He does get things done."

"He looks like an albino gorilla." Ed nodded over the ID. Then Ed grudgingly added, "His features are a bit better." Ed's eyes narrowed. "He looks like a crook. Have you done a background check on him?"

"You'd hurt his feelings if you said something like that to him. He's very kind and gentle."

"Doing...what?" Ed leaned his head closer to her and his face was stony.

She gestured in a gentle openness as she explained, "His work."

"He doesn't look like a painter."

She raised her eyebrows. "What's a painter look like? You? He doesn't look at all like you." Then she was soothing. "He's another careful worker." To change the subject, she asked Ed, "Have you ever been on one of the riverboats? The ones with gambling?"

"Sure."

"I never have. Did you go on a moored boat or one that went out on the river?"

"Both. They're just like anything else. But on the river, the view's better. And the food's good. Would you like to go?"

She smiled a little as if it was an unexpected invitation—or as if he'd taken the hook? She said, "Yeah. That would be fun."

"Let's go now."

"I'll...check my calendar. Let me call you...in about an hour?"

So she had dismissed him. She hadn't suggested he stay there while she changed. There were two rooms. She could have done that. So he pushed it. "You're dressed just right."

She smiled at Ed. "Thank you. I'll see."

"We haven't had dessert." He said that as he looked at her. Why would she want him out of her place…for an hour?

She said, "We can have dessert on board the boat."

That was logical, but hadn't she prepared any dessert? Hmmmm. And his mind went searching. It landed on the big lump who had checked on her.

However, Ed replied slowly, "Okay. Call me. Do you have my number?"

Her eyes twinkled, so amused, and she replied, "Yes."

She did have his phone number—and his parents' number. That was nigglingly interesting.

As Ed was putting his arms into his jacket, he noticed that her binoculars weren't in sight in her temporary apartment. She had either put them away or kept them in the other apartment so that she could take breaks and look around.

Her curiosity was interesting. Ed had never before seen any painter who cared about anything but getting the job done and going on to another.

And she was slow.

Quick to get phone numbers, but a slow painter.

As directed, Ed left the apartment and drove back to his place at the compound. He was somewhat disgruntled because he didn't understand her wanting the break in their time together. Why had he had to leave her?

And again he considered that while her apartment was being painted, by her, her interim place was a two-room apartment. If she'd wanted to change clothes, she could have closed the bedroom door. He wouldn't have been offended by that.

She just didn't add up.

Maybe she was married to that lump of a lug. However, he didn't appear to be the tolerant type. Was she dating the guy? And she needed permission to take off for a night out with another man? Hardly. She wouldn't be involved with a guy like that lump.

But the guy had really looked Ed over. He'd been so hostile that Ed was surprised the guy hadn't sat down on the sofa and read the paper until Ed left.

There'd been daddies who'd done that when Ed was young and dating younger girls who were not yet women.

Daddies had it rough.

How strange for Ed to think of that at this time. Marcia was old enough to date without having a chaperone. From the looks of her, she wasn't a newly born chick. She'd been around a block or two.

Marcia had the look of a woman who had seen life and survived it very well. She had moxie. She knew what was what. Who was who. And she was familiar with the ropes that set off conduct.

How interesting that she had so carefully shunned Ed...almost. She'd had lunch with him twice and barely said a word either of those times. She'd talked before then when they'd first met. But during those two lunches, she'd hardly said anything.

This time, at her own place, she'd been quite chatty. And it had been *she* who had brought up the gambling boats!

She'd probably borrow money in order to play the slots "one more time." Yeah, she'd be like that.

Gamblers probably had a welcome mat they put out just for her. They'd hired her to bring in new blood—him—for their gambling.

She was a touter. They probably gave her extra chances. Not money. She'd spend that anyway.

Ed considered his cynicism. Well, he'd also been around the block a time or two. After all, he was thirty-seven. In a couple of years he'd be edging into—forty! By that age, a man had been around and seen and experienced just about everything.

And he knew women.

Yes, he did.

Ed paced his floor and waited for her call. Why would he be that impatient? He ought to sit down and read the paper and be as aloof as she deserved.

His phone rang and instead of letting it ring at least twice, he grabbed it right away. A really stupid thing to do with a new woman. He said a casual, "Hello." What a stupid thing to say. Why hadn't he said, "I'm here." Or "It took you long enough."

A male voice said, "Ed? This is Charlie. You busy?"

God, Charlie was the world's worst chatterer. Why had he called then?

So Ed replied quickly, "I'm waiting for a call from California. Let me get back to you."

And Charlie said, "Well..."

But Ed hung up.

And the phone rang!

Cautiously Ed said, "Yeah?"

She said, "Come by in twenty minutes?"

Ed replied, "Yeah."

She hung up.

He was slower.

Being ready, Ed needed to delay about fifteen minutes, so he called Charlie. Ed began, "I got just under fifteen minutes. Give me an outline."

"How'd you know?"

"What! How'd I know what?" Ed frowned at the wall.

"My job's been eliminated in the downsizing of the company."

"Uh-oh."

"We've got four kids!"

"Didn't you ever expect this to happen?"

Charlie reminded Ed, "My father-in-law was the senior executive vice president."

Carefully, Ed echoed, "Was?"

"Yeah."

"Why don't you two come to our meeting on Wednesday. It's a great support group and—"

"Jim is zonked. He can't face it."

"I'll give you a list of the members tomorrow. He'll be right at home. It'll be a shock to see the numbers and caliber of those present. Have heart."

"Ed—"

"I have a new date in five minutes. I'll get back to you tomorrow. Chins up. This is solvable. You'll be astounded. Hang in there." And Ed hung up.

If he hadn't hung up, it would have been a crying jag next. While that isn't wrong for a man to be shocked in such a matter, it was wrong for Ed to be involved in it right at that minute.

He had given the first glimmer of light in the end of the dark tunnel for Charlie—and probably his father-in-law. Tomorrow, Ed would listen as long as it took Charlie to get the pus out of the aching wound of surprise at being fired.

The word had once been terminated. That had sounded so final. Like a death knell.

Released was another substitute word for fired. The mental image was pigeons being freed from a sack on a rooftop.

Being fired was now called downsizing. That meant the firm was in trouble financially. The CEOs were paid too much in unbelievably staggering amounts. That took money from the budget, which limited or shrunk the lower echelon.

Charlie was Ed's age, give or take a couple of years. He was a good, easy golfer and a cheerful father. His father-in-law was a competent man and had been hanging on carefully by his fingernails. At his age, he was mistaken for deadwood.

The company would hire some cheap, wet-eared kids, and those novices would proceed to brilliantly foul things up. Then the older men would be brought back on piecework to try to sort out and glue the whole mess together while the kids learned what to do.

It was all as inevitable as rain. Sometimes it took longer but it would rain.

Then Ed remembered reading in *Time* magazine of the archaeologists who had dug into the soil of the Middle East. They discovered that once there had been a three-*hundred*-year drought.

A stunning thing. There were no seeds in those soil layers of time. The land had been stark and barren.

So as Ed went out to his car to go pick up Marcia, his thoughts of the offer in California loomed in his mind.

At least Ed had an income. Forewarned is really forearmed. If he hadn't "downsized" his own life, he'd be in the same bind Charlie now found himself.

But Ed had caught the wind shift for middle management. He'd studied how to counter it. And now he knew he would be all right. With study, anything can be stabilized.

In time, even Charlie and his father-in-law would be okay. They might not have the clout they'd had, but they'd be all right. They'd be back on the treadmill.

Treadmill.

That was an interesting word to pop up at such a time. Did Ed consider that working in an office was a...treadmill? Had he been doing altered things over and over, from varying directions, and mentally getting nowhere? Hmmmm.

Was there a glass roof for men? Yeah. Long before women hit it, there had been men splattered against it.

Being "freed to follow other avenues" was a premise to be considered. At least Ed had no wife and kiddies to worry about.

Ed missed the drollness of the last thought as he arrived at the apartment house to fetch Marcia.

She was dressed in a demure, ladylike, light blue dress. She looked so sweet that she could be the choir director. She could, if the observer didn't notice her sly eyes.

As Ed noticed them, her eyes cleared and the lashes lifted to look into his with honest candor.

This was a woman a man needed to be careful about. She could be dangerous to a man...to him...to Edgar Hollingsworth.

Well, he could handle a little danger.

Ed smiled and said, "You really look different lately. I think it could have been those coveralls."

"Oh, do you suppose?"

"I didn't realize you were...so female."

"You'd never make a cop. No imagination at all." She smiled, her teeth in her lower lip, and her eyes sparkled unduly.

She didn't think he had any imagination? But he replied to her comment, "I've only known pragmatic cops."

Marcia sassed, "They hide their humor and intelligence quite well."

"How do you know that?"

She looked surprised. "I ran into a cop...just this week. It was a fluke, of course."

"Of course."

"But he said I'd turned wrong."

Ed guessed, "It was a one-way street?"

She nodded soberly. "I went into the middle lane and had to back up for almost a mile on the thruway."

Ed nodded serious bobs. "That was an experience. A challenge."

She complained, "A lot of people honked at me."

Again Ed's head nodded in agreement. "That's probably what they'd do."

"A cop came along and led me."

"Well! That was nice."

She explained, "It was so it could be he who gave me the...the lecture! He was really...upset."

"He didn't want you wasted."

She defended herself. "Nobody was shooting at me, only honking."

"You're beautiful."

"I was in my painting coveralls and hat and wearing my glasses. He was not charmed by me...at all."

"Did you drive yourself home?"

She was emphatic. "With great care."

Keeping his eyes mostly on the road, Ed briefly glanced at her as he reached over and waggled her head. "I'm glad you weren't hurt. The cop was probably sweating and worried and a father. Fathers tend to get upset when kids get in physical trouble and come out of it safely."

She countered that. "I broke a fingernail."

It took him a while to realize that was a bad thing. He asked kindly, "Which one?"

She held out her left hand and pointed to the little finger.

With his eyes on the road, he took her hand in his big one and lifted it to his mouth to kiss it. Then he put her hand on his thigh and covered it entirely with his bigger hand, holding it there. It was their first romantic encounter.

Yeah. He'd kissed her finger. But she hadn't withdrawn her hand. Her hand was on his thigh under his hand, and hers wasn't squirming to get away.

What would she do if he put his hand on her thigh? He'd see.

He drove across the bridge over the Illinois River and into East Peoria, which is a manufacturing area. There were hotels and motels along the riverbank. And he drove north to the parking lot for the gambling boats. There was an off-duty cop working the entrance of the big pavilion.

The cop scowled at Marcia.

Ed looked at Marcia. She was old enough. Why the scowl?

As they walked on by the cop and entered the pavilion, Ed glanced back at the cop who was looking off, away, in a rather pointed manner.

Ed asked Marcia, "Who's the cop? Do you know him?"

"He's the one who objected to my going backward down the thruway."

"A stickler." Ed nodded in agreement with his words.

"The worst kind."

Ed was holding the hand with the shortened fingernail.

With other arrivals, the couple came to the split halls in the building. One way was to the dining room. Ed asked, "Would you like dessert here? I don't believe they serve any dessert on board."

Marcia replied, "Not now. I want to see the boat. That would be dessert enough for me."

So they went down the other hall. At one of the wire-enclosed cashier cages, Ed paid for tickets to board the gambling boat.

They went up some stairs and then up the covered gangplank and on to the first deck. There were open covered decks on each level and a big paddle wheel was at the back of the boat.

They walked around so that Marcia could see everything.

Ed mentioned, "I can't believe you've never been here before. If you don't gamble, it isn't expensive."

"Who'd come to a gambling boat and not gamble?"

"Me."

She frowned. "How can you not?"

He opened his hand out and replied, "I watch people lose money."

"Some win."

"Not very many."

Off the top deck, inside, there was a big gambling room with specific kinds of gambling. From the lower deck they found an oval bar in the middle of the slot machine room. A sandwich bar was to one side.

First the venturing pair went strolling around, hand in hand, along the open decks. The boat left the mooring and went upriver. Being on a wide river is a pleasure.

She told Ed, "We all love water because we came from the sea."

"I hadn't realized that."

She scoffed, "What a neutral reply."

He held her hand between them and glanced at her tolerantly. It was a beautiful night. A special time. There was a moon.

They mostly watched the water's wake, the turning of the large wheel at the back of the boat, and they watched each other.

Then they went into the gambling rooms to see what all was offered. They watched some of the high rollers. Neither had an alcoholic drink. She asked, "Don't you drink booze?"

"On occasion."

She nodded thoughtfully. And finally they went to gamble.

Ed stopped at a wire cage where he bought and gave her chips. And he watched her play.

She asked, "Aren't you going to play?"

He repeated, "I don't gamble." Of course, he was doing that in looking for a job. He was even gambling with knowing this puzzling woman. She was a painter who painted so gently and precisely that she'd never make a living on her own.

He asked, "Have you been living at home?"

Her eyes concentrated on the machine in front of her, she replied, "How did you know?"

"I was trying to figure how you could afford an apartment. Have you been living with somebody?"

"No. Just at home, as you guessed."

"Never been married?" Why had he asked again? She replied, "No."

What a final word. Why hadn't she said, "Not yet" instead?

Ed looked at her playing the slots. She was so intense, pitted against a programmed machine that way. Why couldn't she be that intense with him?

He was jobless and leaving town.

She didn't know that.

She thought he was employed as the rent collector.

* * *

Well, she hadn't realized he was seeing to the renovation of two places. She only knew he was involved in one. The apartment building.

Once he got all the apartments in shape, he'd be able to get them all rented. Then he'd have a real outfit monitor the rent mailed to them or find out why it wasn't mailed.

It had been a shame the previous, absentee owner hadn't kept the property up. Of course, if it had been, Ed wouldn't have gotten such a good deal on buying it. He'd used the building's deterioration as a lever.

The absentee owner had used it as a tax break.

Ed's dad had helped Ed with the dickering. His dad's helping had made Ed wonder if he'd ever be as smart as his dad.

Of course, there'd been a time—some years back— when he'd thought his father was really out of step and blank.

It was amazing how much the old man had learned in the relatively short time since then. That old saw. But it had seemed true at the time.

Ed looked at the intense female slot player putting in coins and punching the button. Why was she so interesting to him? Why was it she who caught his eye and stirred his sex? Why did he feel the need to cosset her, to protect and guard her?

Really? He did? Yeah.

Well, what it really meant was that he'd like to get her into bed. There wasn't anything awesome going on there, it was just sex. He wanted her. He wanted her naked and breathy and squirming under his body, clawing at his back and trying to get him closer.

And he just might get her. She was proving that she was a gambler.

In some surprise, he noticed that she was piling up quite a lot of the boat's gambling coins.

Then she took out a wisp of a scarf from her purse. She scooped all the collected fake coins into the scarf and gave the small bundle to Ed.

She said to Ed, "Here, hold this. Don't give me any more than twenty-five. Keep count."

But her good luck continued.

And the amazing thing was, she called the halt! She said, "That's enough for now. I have only one more of their coins."

She put it into the slot and pushed the button... and hit the jackpot!

She went wild! She hugged herself, she laughed, she hugged Ed and she shook her head and just laughed.

The people around her watched, frozen-faced or smiling, depending on their attitude.

Ed grinned and willingly hugged her back and helped her scoop up the pile. Then with some prissiness and elaborate indication of good sportswomanship, Marcia put in one coin to get the one-armed bandit back into business.

They took the cache to the wired cage of the boat cashier, and she was given the choice of a check or the cash. Marcia took the cash. With what she'd already won and the jackpot, she had over three hundred dollars.

She turned her back and put it down, inside the front of her dress. A foolish woman.

So they walked out onto the boat's lower deck. She took Ed's hand and couldn't stop her grin. Her eyes sparkled and she laughed at nothing at all but the fact that she had the money in her hand.

Well, down her dress.

They walked around, holding hands and talking. They leaned on the rail and watched the water being pushed aside by the boat. And the boat eventually went back to the dock.

She never once thought to repay Ed for the funding he'd given her to begin it all. She just didn't even think of it.

They'd walked out of the big shore building toward the stony-faced cop. He watched them come along by him. She told the cop, "I won!"

He replied, gruffly disapproving, "This time."

He was not a gambler.

But Marcia was full of herself and just walked along sassily and grinning as she swung Ed's hand and laughed.

He tried to think of other ways she could win.

He was going to kiss her. Where would it lead? She was no neophyte. She had to be older than twenty-five. She looked honed. She looked as if she'd seen Life and knew the score.

He'd let her "score" with him.

* * *

In the car, he would glance over at her as they drove. Would she be so grateful tonight? On their first date? It was the dream of any man.

He lost some hope when she said good-night as she slid out of the car. He got out on the other side and said, "I'll see you to your door."

She stopped and waited for him. There was a strange little smile on her face, and her eyes weighed him.

He understood that he was being judged. That meant he could probably kiss her at the door, but he wouldn't be allowed inside her place. Not then.

Well, maybe another time...

6

As they walked up the first flight of steps at the apartment house, Ed adjusted his voice to the time and the fact resident people were asleep. He told her softly, "When you said you were a painter, I thought you did paintings of pictures."

"No. I flunked art from first grade."

He gestured to communicate. "I . . . we thought we might use some of your pictures on the hall walls."

She readily suggested, "I have a friend—"

"Yeah, so do I. He paints with drips, squiggles and swirls."

"She doesn't. She's realistic and paints all sorts of things. She hasn't picked any particular subject on which to concentrate. She paints what interests her. And she's not very expensive. Why don't you allow her to hang her pictures here with the price tag on them and see if they sell?"

He was more cautious. "I'll ask."

He didn't say who he'd ask. He just didn't want Marcia to know he owned the place . . . plus the other one.

They passed the door of the apartment that was so slowly being painted. He noted the door was closed. They went on past the closed door to her temporary habitation.

He took her key from her hand and opened her door for her. He turned and gave her key back as he looked down at her. He really wanted a kiss. Or a dozen. Why her?

She smiled and said, "Thank you for the evening. It was great!"

He thought how much greater it could be. But he didn't say anything. He did bite his lip very briefly and said, "Thanks for your good company. Good night."

And he kissed her. He leaned his head down, and she didn't move back, so he just went on and kissed her. It was only then, during the distraction of his kiss, that he put his arms around her. His arms were very much like sly, double boa constrictors.

With the kiss, she wouldn't notice he was holding her against his body. Mmmmm. Up close. She was so soft.

Slowly, but with some smothered breathing, he re-slanted his mouth and gathered her closer. He moved one hand down her back to pull her against him.

She evaded his move quite adroitly, but she continued with the kiss.

When he then settled into a serious communication in the kissing, she moved her head and broke the contact.

It was a very skilled counteraction. She'd done that just as he was settling in, ready to push the door open and lift her over inside the apartment.

She broke the kiss quite easily and leaned back with her hands on his chest. Her forearms held him back. She smiled.

What an amused smile.

She ticked him. She'd very skillfully countered him. And she smiled about it. She didn't laugh out loud or scoff. She just smiled in a twinkling humor.

He pretended he'd intended ending the kiss as he said, "You're good company."

"So are you. I had such a nice time."

"We could do something else." He smiled in an innocent manner.

She wasn't dumb. She straightened and moved as she indicated that she wanted him to let her go.

He released her without any problem as if he'd planned to release her right then anyway.

She was amused.

Women are like that. Frustrated men reply with heady smiles and much good humor. He said, "Go on inside and let me be sure your door locks properly."

He knew damn well it did. He'd double-checked all the doors. His master key to the doors' locks was in his pocket. Even if she locked the door, he could get inside. He doubted she knew that. She'd just think he was being purely solicitous.

She had a sliding bolt. She read him like a book. Or a picture. Or a man.

And he was certainly a man. She took a deep breath. She smiled up at the frustrated man. She said, "Good night." And damned if she didn't close the door!

He stood there, recovering somewhat. Well, at least he'd gotten in a really deep kiss. She wouldn't be able to sleep. Not right away.

Then, as he walked carefully to the top of the stairs, he considered that not only did he have to go all the way back to his complex, he had to face a run to calm down.

Women were a marvelously concocted nuisance.

When God had gotten around to making women, He had been very skilled. Men were so simply made and their thinking was so basic. Think of the challenge God had in making a woman!

Or maybe women really *had* come there from another planet. Think how entertained and challenged women were in coping with a simple, straightforward man. Just communicating basics with a man must be heady for them.

How entertaining for a woman to lead a man along and allow him to share her life . . . her way, of course. Ed mulled that over all the way down the stairs to the first floor.

Driving to the complex, Ed considered that it would be worth the time it took to train her right. Of course, he would be leaving for California. But she'd be smoothed enough for another man with most of the work already done.

At the compound, he drove his car into his roofed slot, which was at an angle from his front door. Then he went inside and changed into jogging clothing. He went out and ran.

No man can run from the lure of a woman.

Running only lulls his agitation enough so that he believes he's in control again.

It was interesting that Ed understood the genders so well.

He got back to his place and listened to the various messages left on his phone tape. He wrote notes on some. It was too late at night to reply to others.

Charlie had called again. Ed was very tempted to call and let the guy talk. But there was the chance Charlie was finally asleep. It would be wrong to waken him. If he talked then, how could Ed soothe Charlie enough that he could go back to sleep?

Ed showered and stood in the hot spray a long time, relaxing. He would sleep. And he did. But his dreams were getting hotter.

Why her?

He wakened to a wrecked bed. He was disgruntled. He looked at the chaos and thought only teenagers messed up a bed that way.

It had been a long time since his libido was so triggered. It must be his second adolescence. Hell. To go through all that again? Surely not.

In the trashed bed, Ed lay with his hands behind his head as he stared at the ceiling. He would conquer this strange attraction and not see her for a week.

Satisfied that he was again in control, Ed got up and stripped the bed. Pitching the bedding and pad into a pile, he remade the bed in a precise, masculine no-nonsense, utilitarian manner.

Then he scrubbed himself in the shower and dressed in jeans and a short-sleeved T-shirt. He fixed himself a good hot breakfast of cereal, toasted waffles, fruit and milk.

He took his clothes bag and the bag with the bedding to the laundry and filled two machines. He then asked the supervisor to take them out when they were done and fold them. He paid for that.

She smiled at him. She was probably closer to his age and would be easier. He was businesslike but kind.

The day was overcast. The catfish were more active when it was cloudy or if there was a slight rain. They would bite better. They did because the rain brought the insects down to the water.

So he asked Rudolf and Amy if he could rent their boat.

Rudolf replied, "We took you with us. Are you going to invite us along?"

"No."

Rudolf's eyes glinted. His voice was mournful. "Today's a fishing day. We could catch a bunch of catfish, and Amy would cook them."

Amy said, "They'd be great on a charcoal grill. You cook them. I'll make a slaw salad."

Ed mentioned, "I'd like to have a peaceful trip without all your chatter."

Rudolf turned to his wife. "Remember before we was married?"

Ed was patient. "I'm not going to marry Marcia, we're just going fishing."

Both of the Smiths laughed.

Ed looked at them in real puzzlement. "That's all."

The couple thought that was hilarious!

Still laughing, Rudolf gave the boat keys to Ed. He slapped Ed on the shoulder a couple of hilarious times. He mumbled things Ed didn't get, but the old man sure did laugh.

Then Rudolf cautioned, "No hanky-panky on the boat. It's a virgin."

Friends can be a trying nuisance at the worst of times.

Ed went to the apartment building and up the stairs to her apartment. She did not answer his knock. He went to the apartment she was painting, but the door was closed. Ed tried it. And it, too, was locked!

He inserted his master key, and it did not unlock the door! It should have. He'd had it fixed! What the hell had she done? And why? To again change the lock on an empty apartment was not logical.

A new lock on one of his apartments did not sit well on Ed's shoulders. What was she doing?

After all, he considered the fact, she *was* Elinor's renter. Any connection anyone might have with the tricky and elusive Elinor should make a man wonder about her. How close *was* Marcia to that tricky, unlawful, sneaky Elinor?

He'd just find out. He sat on the top step of the staircase and wondered where she was and how long she'd be gone?

And the door into the building opened. Someone walked in. The steps were heavier than a woman's. Who was it?

It was the janitor who had been hired by Ed's predecessor. He was doing a better job of it now. His steps were lighter and quicker.

Well, sure. He'd seen Ed's car parked outside.

Ed sat there on the stairs for over an hour. It was a stupid, juvenile thing to do. He grimly sat. He ought to be back at his place and talking to Charlie.

He should.

He went back and knocked on both doors. Her temporary place gave no reply. Her partially painted apartment door was opened by the lump who asked, "Yeah?"

"Where's Marcia?"

"I don' know."

He started to close the door, but Ed put his foot into the opening and asked, "Did you change the lock on this door?"

"Not me."

"It's been changed. That's illegal. It has to be changed back."

"I'll take care of it." Then he told Ed, "Women are different. She probably feels insecure painting up here all by herself."

"What are you doing here?" A logical question.

"My old lady threw me out. I'm negotiating."

From "throwed" to "negotiating"? An interesting mix.

Ed narrowed his eyes at the lump. But the lump only stared.

There was nothing else Ed could do at that time and with that association. So he bobbed his head once, turned and walked away.

He'd learned nothing. Where was she? She was supposed to be painting so that she could pay the down payment on her apartment.

And while she was doing that, she was occupying two apartments. Not only that, but the lump was in one. And the lock had been changed.

Ed suspected he wasn't in control.

Then he went back and knocked again on the lump's door. It was patiently opened, after a time, and the lump just stared. Ed didn't blame the guy. He said, "When Marcia comes back, would you ask her to call Ed?"

And the lump replied, "Sure." But the word could well have been mockery.

So Ed said, "Get the lock changed back."

"We will."

Ed left. As he went down the series of stairs, he contemplated the "we will" of the lump's reply. They would...what?

When he got home, Ed went to his phone to call Charlie, but he hesitated. If he was on the phone, he wouldn't get Marcia's call.

He paced around and the phone didn't ring. He stared at it. Then he went out and drove over to Charlie's. If Charlie needed to talk, Ed could listen then. Or they could go for a cup of coffee and Charlie could unload some of his worry then.

Charlie wasn't home. June was a little distracted. She just stood and waited until it finally dawned on Ed that Charlie was not there and June didn't want to chat.

Finally Ed went back to his place. And there was, indeed, a message from Marcia. She said, "Hi. I'm shopping. Tim said you wanted to talk to me. I'll be back at the apartment about three. Bye."

He changed into other clothing and went out on Rudolf's boat alone. He didn't fish. He considered the world, its inhabitants, the times, the manners and mores. He solved nothing.

He returned the boat on time. He told Rudolf it was a good, head-clearing outing, and he mentioned the fact he went alone.

At three, Ed was at the apartment house. He felt like a fly on a spider's string, which was pulling him into the web. Entrapment.

Naw. Nothing like that. He just wanted... Well, he was just curious... For some strange reason, he needed to see that lousy painter.

What possible excuse could he have?

He couldn't think of a one. What good would it do to stand in Marcia's door and allow his tongue to stumble around while he concocted some excuse for hounding after her?

Ed considered just who was in charge of his actions. His brain or his hungry body? He suspected it wasn't his brain.

So he went down to the basement and shifted things around and got all dirty and sweaty. He figured the exercise was good for him and more productive than a run down the river road.

He went out for supper and ate alone. He called Charlie. Charlie invited him over for dessert. So Ed went over there.

And Ed listened as Charlie told him what a good employee he'd been and asked why had he been eliminated? He hadn't done anything wrong! Nothing but the MacGuire file. But that shouldn't have sunk his whole career!

Ed mentioned, "It wasn't the MacGuire file. That was ten years ago. That was salvaged. Don't let it—"

"Then, why?"

And Ed replied, "Downsizing."

"But why...me?"

He was very vulnerable. And Ed began Charlie's recovery. "Do you remember the Oxford file?"

And Charlie did smile. It was a pale version of his hearty laugh, but it was a smile.

So Ed was there with Charlie for a long time. When the kids were in bed, June came in and quietly sat, listening.

Since the two men had worked in the same echelon instead of separate ones, Ed had a lot of morale boosting material to help Charlie look at himself in another way. Not as a failure.

And Ed began to strengthen Charlie's opinion of himself. They talked of other people they knew who were in the same boat. And Ed mentioned Rudolf's boat. After that, they talked fishing.

Charlie wasn't healed, but he'd been distracted. He promised to go to the research meeting on Wednesday.

It was a long evening. It was all familiar to Ed. He went back to his place wrung out. There were messages on his machine. One was from Marcia.

She had said, "Will you join me for supper on Wednesday?"

Wednesday.

And he was so tempted. It would be such a break in his cluttered life to sit and just look at Marcia. Why her?

He called her and told *her* answering machine. "I'm tied up on Wednesday. How about Thursday or Friday?" And he flinched because he was free two days in a row.

Then he thought: Did that matter? Wasn't he old enough to be honest? Why *not* let her know he was free for her?

Free... for her? What was he thinking? A jobless man! A jobless man didn't get involved with a woman until he had a job and could take care of her.

She sure couldn't take care of him. Not the way she painted. The slow way she painted, no wonder she'd been living at home.

The way she'd been brought up and as long as she'd stayed at home, she was probably still a virgin. A virgin? Did they still have—virgins? Naw!

Ed wasn't there when she left the next message. She said, "I would be pleased to share your company for dinner on Thursday at six o'clock. Signed, Marcia."

She was getting sassy. That was because he'd given her two free days to choose from. Well, he liked women to be a little sassy. He'd let her practice on him before he left Peoria and went off to California.

So.

He was going to go to California? That was something of a surprise to Ed. When had his brain come to that decision? On what grounds? Ed couldn't recall any inner debate. The last he knew, he'd discarded the idea. Had the decision been made in his time with Charlie?

And there was the fact that all his family lived around Peoria. Both sides of his parents were still there. That was very unusual. Most people's families were scattered all over everywhere and didn't even know each other.

If he left Peoria and moved to California, would they all come visiting him? Probably. They'd say, *Well, it was just a good time to come out here and look around, since we can stay free with you. What's for supper?*

His relatives were that exact way.

Had his subconscious realized they were that way and decided on its own that Ed would leave? It had been a rash decision of his subconsciousness to make such a choice.

What would he say when people asked him why he'd gone to California? How could he respond *I don't know* even if it was the truth?

On Wednesday evening, the gathering of the unemployed shared their varying ideas. They discussed what might be done. And they listened to the new ones who do have to have time to grieve and heal.

Most of them, having been in the group for a while, weren't that patient. "You'll thank your stars one day because you had another opportunity."

And "Look at Phil! Who'd ever guess he had the ability to solve that little, folding company? He's saved them all, and they think he's a miracle!"

And "Jim had never known he just needed the time to paint those remarkable pictures! He's—"

Ed asked, "What pictures?"

And Jim said, "Come over tomorrow and see."

"I have a dinner date."

Jim suggested, "Come ahead or bring your dinner partner along?"

"I'll bring her along."

So that changed the subject. They whooped and hollered and asked Ed all sorts of impertinent, outrageous questions about his new woman.

Ed shook his head and chided the group. He *tsked* and was shocked. But he felt his anger rising and that did startle him.

The one woman there finally said quite sternly, "That's enough!"

While the men chuffed and snorted, they did settle down.

The woman said, "What about me? What can I do that will earn me a living?"

Oddly enough no one mentioned the automatic response. They settled down and discussed what all she could do with the excellent talents she'd attained while she'd bumped against the glass roof. And there were good suggestions.

On Thursday at six, Ed went to Marcia's temp apartment. She was dressed in a lovely new suit. It was a dark raspberry. She wore no blouse under the jacket. Her shoes were a darker, almost black raspberry.

She looked like a dream woman.

Ed wasn't wearing a jacket or tie. He'd thought they were eating at her apartment as they had the last time.

Obviously, he was supposed to take her out. With that outfit on, he was pleased to do so.

Ed escorted her down the stairs and out to his car. He smiled at her and said, "I have to stop by my place for a tie and jacket. I can't go this way."

She tilted her head and said, "Okay."

That she would go to his place wasn't that surprising, but asking her there and having her agree was an aphrodisiac. How odd.

She loved the compound. She exclaimed over the center tree and the view of the Illinois River down below. And she loved his segment.

While he changed, she went around his other rooms and picked up things to look at them. A vase. A book. A plaque. It had been for running in school.

When he came into the living room still tying his tie and carrying his coat jacket under one arm, she said, "So you can run."

He lowered his eyelashes enough and confirmed it, "I'm thirty-seven and still running—away." He'd said something like that for about ten years. And as usual, he laughed.

She didn't laugh. She looked at him and exclaimed, "Thirty-*seven?*"

Uh-oh.

And he had the gall to inquire, "How old are you? Or should I ask, how young are you?"

She was standing there, very serious faced, and she replied soberly, "I'm forty."

He said, "Oh," as a smile began.

She looked disgusted and told him, "I'm twenty-three."

"Is that all?"

She blinked once. "How old did you think?"

"You're so smooth and handle yourself so well that I assumed you'd be closer to my age than twenty-three. What is the count—really?"

She shrugged. "I'm twenty-three."

"How old did you think I was?"

"I figured you were probably thirty at the oldest."

He had finished his tie and was shrugging into his suit jacket. "Are you really only twenty-three?"

"Yes."

"Well, I have a cousin that might be okay for you."

"That's only fourteen years. You don't know that much more than I."

He looked at the budding woman with some adult tolerance. "By the time a man is fourteen, he's grown."

She tilted back her head and looked at him from under sophisticated eyelids. "So's a woman."

"Honey, by the time you were fourteen, I was twenty-eight!"

She considered him and had the audacity to mention, "You've aged well."

There is nothing like a sassy-mouthed woman.

He said, "Come on, child, let's go have supper." Then he stopped and asked urgently, "You *can* feed yourself?"

And she took a steadying breath of adult endurance.

7

As they approached his car, Ed told Marcia, "I'll put you inside. And I'm not giving you any lessons in driving a car. Watch. You can learn—on your daddy's car."

She was forbearing.

As they stopped at a traffic light, a guy standing on the corner smiled at Marcia. She didn't blush or whip her head away or wiggle or giggle.

Ed had the gall to compliment her. "You handle yourself quite well."

"Thanks."

"That didn't sound at all sincere."

"Are we going through a whole evening of adult/child innuendos?"

"That's a salacious word."

She frowned at him. "What word?"

He smiled and licked his lips. She was really innocent. Well, it was a change. Let's see. How did a male talk to a nubile female?

He communicated, "I'm in a different generation from your *next* generation. What are the bursting-into adulthood conduct and fashions now?"

"About like always." The sound of her voice was patient. Then, with her eyes slid sideways in a droll look, she added, "We don't wear helicopter blades on beanie caps."

He nodded soberly and corrected, "We didn't, either. That was before us."

"It's coming back. There was one at the Woodstock '94."

"Did you go?"

"No." Then she asked kindly with lifted eyebrows, "Were you there at the first one?"

"My mother wouldn't let me and Dad backed her." After a calculating pause, he had the gall to state, "You weren't even *born* then."

She slid it in, "You were eleven? Twelve?"

He sighed. "Yeah. And I missed it all. The one in '94 was too commercial."

"The next one will probably be in New Mexico. Patty will orchestrate it."

"Patty?"

"Patricia Gardner Evans. A remarkable writer and an elegant doer. She'd manage it easily, but without all the hype and commercialism. She'd probably study up on it and personally string all the electrical wires...safely. And it probably wouldn't rain out there."

Ed nodded as he watched the street's hazards of cars and peoples. He observed to his passenger, "I know it rained the first Woodstock, and the one in '94, but I suspect it also rained during the twenty-five years in between."

"Yes."

He grinned over at the budding woman and said, "You're agreeable?"

"I believe the word is 'courteous' and has no real acquaintance with manners." She looked at him with forbearance.

Back to watching where his car was heading, Ed nodded in courtesy and said, "Your mother did a good job on your manners."

"She's about your age."

Since the new woman was so snippy and unrattled about his hazing conduct, he turned his head and smiled at her.

She was looking out the window.

His chuckle rumbled in his chest.

She sighed and inquired in a top-lofty manner, "Well, Uncle Ed, where are you taking me?"

"To my dungeon."

She rolled her head in loose endurance of circumstance. "One of those."

"It'll be a widening experience." He promised her.

But he pulled into the parking lot of an elegant new restaurant. It was discreetly identified as Joe's. Who had been so droll?

Ed got out as her door was opened by a bowing, uniformed doorman. A parking attendant was already holding the door for Ed. The attendant slid into the car and drove the ordinary car off to park it among the more remarkable gathering of cars.

Ed joined Marcia and escorted her into the restaurant. It was a very posh place. The maître d' led them to a good table. Then the waiter came to give the couple their menus. Hers did not show the price of anything. The wine steward listened as Ed consulted with him on the wines.

Everything was perfectly done. The couple argued all the way through their elegant dinner courses, which he had ordered for her. He said, "You'll have to try this."

When that course was served, she asked, "What is it?"

"How do you like it?"

"It tastes . . . different."

"It's squid."

"Oh."

But she did eat it. He was impressed. He smiled at her and was pleased that she had the gall to go ahead and eat something so different.

She observed him with tolerance.

He asked, "How can you act so adult at twenty-three?"

"I was trained to be adult . . . in school."

"I suppose we are all adult but generally women don't have to mature as young as men. No. No...I meant no insult. I am complimenting you."

She rejected his explanation. "That is very similar to replying either yes or no to the question, 'Have you quit beating your wife?'"

He grinned. "That old saw."

"Men never recognize that females are equal to them...when women go to such lengths to allow men to fool they are equal." She looked at Ed pacifically.

He loved it. "Women are naturally kind. We tend to appreciate it. Especially when we need their admiration to bolster our morale."

She lifted the tiny spoon to freshen her palate with the between-courses sherbet. She responded in confirmation, "We are kind."

And Ed had the feeling that she was, indeed, being very kind to him. That rattled him a little.

He asked, "What are your life's plans?" And when she didn't instantly respond, he moved his left hand in a circle to elaborate, "Marriage and children?"

"How limiting."

Ed laughed. He was so amused. His eyes sparkled and he bit into his lower lip to control his guffaws. "You have larger plans?"

"Yes."

"What?"

His question was a logical one, but it was given in such asininely, indulgently, male adult to nubile female that it irritated the liver out of her. She replied, "I'll see."

He nudged. "After you've tried the painting?"

And she slid it in. "It's a part of the larger picture."

He thought she just meant in painting and he was so amused. "So you're going to do canvases next?"

"I already do. Haven't you noticed the patterns on the drop canvases? They are thrillingly unique, so casual, so unplanned. All I have to do is hang them in the right atmosphere. They'll bring in a fortune."

So he finally knew she was disgruntled with him...maybe. Of course, artists could be strange and she could be communicating with him. He wasn't sure how to reply, so he nodded as if thinking seriously.

She gave him a lowered-in-disgust glance as she turned her head away while still watching such a numbskull.

She'd been leading him along, and he'd been stupid enough to take her seriously.

He said, "You're an interesting study. Have you ever thought seriously of going into business by yourself?"

With exquisite kindness, she replied, "I am—already—in business for myself."

"I really meant in some project that could earn your living."

"It does. "

Her abrupt reply did baffle him. He didn't know how to quiz her on her financial program with the interminable time she took in just painting one apartment. At the rate she was going, she might get nine apartments done in a year. More than likely it would be seven.

Maybe she really was into paint-splattered drop cloths? Nothing surprises a man who is a weighty thirty-seven years old. By then, he's encountered all kinds of peoples. This ethnic, singular "people" across the table from him was a real weirdo.

But she was stimulatingly attractive to any male. And she had his attention. He wanted to initiate her into the ramifications of Life.

Well . . . when had he decided on that?

Probably just about right away, the first time he laid eyes on her as she was moving into the crook Elinor's deserted apartment. How could he tell? Almost immediately, his sex had indicated his interest.

No man should be led around by his sex. That's why a man had a brain. With a brain, he had some control. While he thought that so rejectingly, his eyes were on that nubile woman across the table from him. And his sex was pushy.

No wonder men wore suit coats.

And the woman across the table didn't have a blouse on under her suit coat. She was naked under that cloth.

Probably not. She probably wore a utilitarian cotton slip and an iron bra.

If they danced, the points of the iron bra would probably shred his suit coat and scratch his chest. He asked, "Would you like to dance for a while? It would settle our stomachs, and we could eat more later."

She looked over at the dance floor and listened to the type of music the band was playing. "All right."

He rose as he considered that he should have worn a vest to pad his chest a little more and protect his flesh from the steely points of her iron bra. He managed to get around the table in time to hold her chair back for her.

He escorted her to the small dance floor. Two other couples were moving to the music as they talked.

Ed took Marcia into his arms and found she was the exact right size. Gingerly he drew her closer.

She was so soft.

Ed was so adolescently concentrated on the feel of Marcia in his arms, of her softness against his susceptible body, that he didn't hear her words.

He did know she was talking, but he just silently groaned as he closed his eyes and held her closer.

She said quite clearly, "You're old enough to control such conduct."

How disgustingly mature of her.

She went on, "You're old enough to have a—mature, I believe you labeled yourself, fourteen-year-old of your own."

He pulled back to look at her bland face in some disgust.

She shrugged. "You said you were mature at fourteen. It wouldn't be unheard of for you to have fathered a child at twenty-two."

"I was just graduated from Illinois."

"The state or the university?"

He leaned back a little to regard the mouthy neophyte. He set her straight. "The university."

"What was your major?"

"Business."

"That probably helped you considerably." Then she took her hand from his shoulder and covered her mouth. "I'd forgotten you are a rent collector."

"You have a very nasty way of talking to a man who is buying your supper."

"Here, at this elegant place, it's dinner."

"Yeah. Behave or you split the check."

"I can handle half of it. We'll split it."

There isn't anything more irritating to a controlling man than a freewheeling woman. So he said, "Okay, we'll split it."

"Actually. . ." She studied him with some discarding. "I owe you for funding my gambling. I'll pay the bill."

"Not this time, baby. It was my idea to come here."

She understood the "baby" was not an endearment. She inquired politely, "Are we quarreling?"

"You're so stiff-necked that you're just about impossible."

With mature kindness she corrected him gently. "Not 'just about' but completely. Shall we go back to the table and finish up? I have an early morning tomorrow."

He continued dancing. Well, he didn't let her go and leave the dance floor. He asked, "How could you be on any schedule?"

Without hesitation, she retorted, "I have working hours, just like anyone else."

He laughed. He closed his lips and smothered and bit at the laughter. He couldn't stop and his eyes sparkled and the lights in them danced.

Such laughter is contagious. She grinned.

His arm pulled her closer, and they danced easily without saying anything else. When the set was finished, they went back to their table.

Their waiter inquired, "Dessert?"

And they studied the choices on the menu. It was a tearing choice. They decided on three. They'd share.

Their tolerant waiter whisked on the extra small plates, each with its own fresh dessert fork or spoon. And he served their choices. He lingered and glanced at them and anticipated their delight.

They were delighted. The meringue was sinful. The cookie/ice cream/nut one was outrageously marvelous, and the whipped cream/fruit was wicked.

Neither of the two actually licked their plates. They agreed that showed they were grown-ups. Not licking plates proved their upper echelon of maturity.

And they decided being mature was a real pain.

It took his credit card to cover the cost. He didn't say anything and his tip was just a tad more than expected.

Their car was ready for them at the door. Obviously the waiter had contacted the car jockey. While Ed eased Marcia into her seat, the car jockey held the driver door at ready. And he took his tip slyly and it disappeared quickly into his pocket without his even peeking at it. He was very smooth.

Ed drove his replacement car with easy skill. He headed down toward the river. It was late and the traffic was still busy.

She asked, "You've been...mature...longer. Does it ever get easier?"

"Before I respond to your question, let me wipe the whipped cream from my flowing, gray beard." He looked over at her with amused patience.

She lifted her eyebrows and told him, "I realize that will take a while. You've been a graybeard for so long. Will you kindly repeat my question at the beginning of your response? By then, I just may not remember what I asked of you."

Making his voice wobbly and cracked, Ed replied, "There's nothing worse than a snippy youngster. Hush, child. Your momma won't be pleased with my report on you. You did say this was your first evening out without a chaperone?"

"Yes, sir, Mr. Hollingsworth." Then she looked over at him and said, "That is an elegant name. What was your original last name? The one before this one."

"So. You don't think I'm elegant?"

She replied thoughtfully, "Rather basic, to my scant knowledge. You do know how to bone a fish the neatest I've ever witnessed."

He inquired with curiosity, "Then why did you cut it crossways?"

"I wanted to see what you'd say. You were very brave and quite mature in keeping your shock to yourself."

"Then you do realize a fish is filleted?"

"Honey, we've lived on the Illinois River for a long, long time."

He nodded, accepting that premise, and replied, "We're probably blood kin, if you go back far enough."

"That would certainly shock my mother."

"She doesn't even know me! What have you said about me to her?"

"Nothing!" Marcia was indignant. "If we turned out to be kin, you would want to home in on our family, and you would shock my mother."

"Why?"

"Because you're wicked."

His face went blank and his lips parted just a bit in shock as he glanced over at Marcia. "I've been a perfect gentleman!" Indignation is an excellent barrier. And how could she have read his mind and found out otherwise?

"I've been aware of the sly movements. You've touched me about everywhere . . . by accident."

"They all *were* accidental!"

"So you're aware you've been brushing around on me?"

"I have not! I'm a gentleman!"

"Who says so?"

"My mother."

"A blind woman?"

"No! She's a hovering buzzard of a mother. She watches us like a hawk! You wouldn't believe what a weasel she is in questioning our conduct!"

"Hmmm." She narrowed her eyes. "A hawk, a weasel and a buzzard? Genetically, you're an interesting combination. What influence did your father contribute?"

"He showed us that it's never worth the time to argue. Any man who argues with a woman only gets in deeper. All a guy can do is to just do everything her way and leave the house as soon as he can."

"One of those."

"Dad taught us that a guy can go back again. Just to wait long enough for her to calm down and miss him."

"I believe that is a very stupid thing to do. While she's trying to communicate, you ought to listen to her. You just might learn something. If you keep walking out until the quarrel blows over, you won't really know what's wrong. The quarrel might heal over, but it'll fester and it could burst into a real problem."

He looked over at her. "How'd you get that smart?"

"I'm a woman."

He was silent. He coughed once. He licked his lips. Then he finally glanced over at her. She was sitting in a serene manner, looking out of her window. She had spoken.

He coughed another time or two.

She turned her head slowly and asked with a false concern, "Swallow a bone?"

He laughed as he said, "Probably."

She suggested, "Stop the car and I'll whack you on the back."

"I hesitate to ask on the back . . . of what?"

"How many backs do you have?"

"There's the back of my head, the back of my knees, the back of—"

Prissily, she instructed, "When one chokes, one swats the chokee on the back of his chest."

"Oh."

In a disbelieving tone, she inquired, "You've never done that before?"

"Nobody I know chokes."

"You probably reply differently to those you know well."

"Different . . . from what?"

"Friends who aren't women. My telling you I knew because I am a woman caused you to choke. What have you thought I was? I'm told I do look female."

With some seriousness, he allowed her the tribute. "You think like a man."

"No. I think like a human."

"Do you think men think like . . . humans?"

"Very few. Mostly they just go along thinking like men do."

"In . . . what way?"

"Basics."

Ed thought about that as he drove along with exceptional skill. "Yeah. You got it right. Men do that. On occasion we talk to women just to see how their minds work. It is always a remarkable insight. Women are different."

"I know."

"My place?"

She moved her head in a slow, discarding motion and her mouth was about to form the word no.

Ed saw that and said, "I have a good friend who was recently a victim of company downsizing. I need to check in with him."

"It's almost eleven o'clock."

"He's always been a night owl. He'll be up another hour. He gets to sleep later in the mornings."

"Kids?"

"Yeah."

"And his wife works?"

"Yeah."

"He's feeling abandoned."

"Exactly."

"Okay. But you could just drop me off."

"If I did that, I'd be too late in getting to Charlie."

"Why . . . too late?"

"Well, I spent a lot of money on you to—"

"I'll pay my half."

"—and we need to share the savoring of the various things we ate and discuss them so it was worthwhile to do all that eating. What do you remember especially? No...don't start. I have to call Charlie, first."

"You can call from my apartment."

"Which one?"

"The one I'll be living in."

"Well, I really think it would be better to call Charlie from my place. He's going to want to talk too long, and I can tell him I've got to get you home at a reasonable time."

That sounded logical. Which just proves how sly men can be.

She commented, "As I recall, the apartment house is closest, and you can drop me there first and go on home and let Charlie take his time. He probably needs to get rid of all the distress...like women who need to talk to their husbands."

Ed blinked. Was she teaching him to be a husband? Him? No way. He said, "The call'll only be ten minutes, and we'll have the opportunity to discuss the skill of the chef before it all fades from our palates."

Actually, her nod acknowledged his slyness. Well, what did she expect of a man who was sly and thirty-seven?

Ed drove back to his place. When he came around the car to open her door, the door was locked but she said, "Since it won't take you long, I'll just wait here."

He took his car key out and unlocked her door quite smoothly. He smiled and said, "I don't want to leave you out here alone. You'll be safer inside."

She looked around the calm compound. She slid her eyes over to the probable Mr. Hyde person waiting to take her arm and help her from the shelter of his car.

Inside, she smiled. She was expert in karate. She exited the car. He was past due in finding out about real women.

They entered his dark apartment. She observed mildly, "You ought to have small lights in a socket in each room. Then you wouldn't break a toe or be surprised."

He smiled and reached for her but missed as she moved to a lamp. He got to watch as it turned on. She wasn't *that* young! Well, he'd teach her.

He went to the phone and dialed Charlie's number. Supposedly. He actually dialed the police desk. It was always busy. He got a cop. He said, "Sorry," and redialed Charlie's number.

And *it* was busy!

So he put down the phone and said, "It might take a minute or two." He indicated the sofa and said, "Sit over there by the lamp. The light on your hair is so pretty."

She chose a chair instead. She picked up *Field and Stream* and flipped through it with some casual interest.

He watched her. He knew she would look up eventually and get up out of that chair and come to him, her body starving for his. She'd wrap herself around him like a two-legged boa constrictor. He'd struggle like his mother had always warned, but she would conquer him.

She went on reading.

He knew that she lusted for him but she was being stern with her libido. She hungered for his body. He considered. He hadn't had thoughts like that since he was about . . . fifteen. What was it about her?

He realized she was controlling herself.

Her breathing was slow and calm. How rude of her.

He tried Charlie again. Charlie's phone was still busy. Ed wondered whose shoulder was wet by then? Who was Charlie's other contact? Well, that did make it easier on Ed if Charlie had found another ear to bend with all his problems.

He looked over at the twenty-three-year-old innocent. She was still reading the magazine. How many women read *Field and Stream?* Probably more than he'd ever realized.

He said, "Find something else interesting?"

He expected her to put down the magazine and laugh, but she apparently finished the paragraph and then looked up as she kept her place with one finger. She inquired, "Ready?"

That set off all his idle cells, but then she said, "This is an old issue, you've probably already read it. Do you mind if I borrow it for a couple of days? This article on bass fishing is especially good."

He gave up.

He said, "Charlie's line's busy. I might just as well take you home."

She was already rising from the chair as he talked. No romance in her. She was a dud. Zero.

He deliberately took his car keys from his pocket as if to obey her immediately. He did so in such a manner that she would think he'd brought her there just for the phone call.

Then, as if it had just hit him, he said, "I have a really good liqueur. It will touch your palate so gently that you'll smile."

"Not this time."

How could any woman already twenty-three years old be so dumb?

8

As is only right, Ed told Marcia, "I took you out, fed you and I'm committed to getting you back to—one of your apartments safe and sound. I get a kiss."

She tilted her head back and looked at him soberly from the sides of her eyes and from behind those lashes. She asked, "If I took you out, fed you and used my own car, would I be given a kiss?"

He added, "If you behaved right."

"Have you?"

"Have I—what."

She explained, "Have you behaved properly?"

"Haven't I?"

Since he was standing there, waiting for her to go to his car, he got to see her chest as she shrugged and replied, "So far."

Ed glanced aside discreetly. He'd been taught young by his older brother not to stare at females. Ed growled, "What do you mean 'so far' when you're practically back home again?"

She turned her head as she looked aside. "I'm still in your apartment and not yet home."

He was predictably indignant. "Don't you trust me?" That old hack.

"So far."

He was earnest. "You could be naked, in bed with me and I'd not touch you if you didn't want it."

She picked up her bulky shoulder purse. "Has that worked very often?"

"No." He said, "Quit being so snooty. You are going home."

Walking toward the door, she questioned kindly, "Have I behaved properly?" She had the gall to ask that of him.

"No."

That did surprise her. She laughed.

He complained, "You haven't flirted or wiggled or brushed against me or leaned over to whisper to me or—"

"Whisper?"

"—salaciously," he seriously instructed the neophyte. Then he continued on in listing her faults. "You didn't convulse over my jokes." In a mature voice he explained, "A slight smile doesn't do it. You need to practice. The next guy won't be as tolerant as I am."

"You're . . . tolerant?"

He nodded emphatically. "Killingly." He was sure. "Come on, get in the car, you're almost home, Goldilocks."

"My hair is brown. I live in an apartment."

He instructed her with mature knowledge, "You're too young being off on your own this way. You ought to go back home before some really lecherous guy finds you."

She was so shocked that she put her hand on her uneven chest and gasped, "You're a gentleman?"

"Yeah. Thank your guardian angel that I am."

For some reason, she then tried her damnedest to muffle her spurt of giggles.

He knew that maturity would finally smooth her, but it would be long after he'd left for California. He wouldn't be witness to her metamorphosis. Some other guy would be the luc—the victim.

Ed opened the front door of his place and waited as she took her own sweet time in walking past him and out to the parked car. She carried the magazine as if she was just a friend and would see him again to give it back. Well, he'd finished reading it anyway.

She had the gall to wait until he opened the car door. It was locked. He unlocked it. He watched as she moved and slid her legs and body gracefully into his car.

She could slide under him that same way. She ought to wear fewer clothes. She was probably a virgin. She was any man's nightmare.

Thinking that, he closed her door with just the strength of his hands pressing firmly. Men never realize how much strength they use so casually.

Sitting safely inside his car, she flicked down the lock on the door between them. He was outside. She was safely in his car.

He had the key.

He walked around, unlocked the driver's door and got in. He closed the door, and they were isolated from the rest of the world. She was with him.

Why did he feel so possessive of her? He looked over at her, and she was just a woman.

A frail woman who needed a strong man to protect her... to lead her through the beginnings of adulthood. She needed him. He looked over at her and smiled a little.

He started the car and eased it from the compound. He glanced at her. She was looking at the side street. She looked around a lot, he'd noticed.

Few women kept everything in sight. Marcia was aware of where she was and who all was around. Women... actually, women weren't always that observant.

Was she looking for—another man? Someone other than Edgar Hollingsworth? He wasn't chopped liver. But he was leaving Illinois. He was going to California.

He'd take her back to her apar—to the interim apartment, and he'd let go of her.

How could he "let go" of her when the only time he'd held her was when they were dancing? He looked over at the silent woman. She didn't say much. She could talk, but the way she talked was cheeky and snotty. She thought she was equal to men.

Watching the street, glancing at the sidewalks and the cross streets, Ed also glanced at the silent woman.

Was it her silence that attracted his desire to ruffle her? What caught her attention?

Why should he care? He wasn't interested. Not in her or any other woman. He was going to California. He'd call John the very next day and talk to him. Feel out the job.

He'd like to feel her out. That woman who was over there not two feet away but acting as if she was already safely home.

It must be kind of tough on a woman going out with an unknown man. She'd taken a big risk coming out with a man so much older and more experienced than she. Maybe she was stupid. Then he wondered if she was actually a tramp.

After all, Marcia had the apartment from Elinor. That was a clue as to her contacts. Maybe Marcia would have a couple of men living with her, just like Elinor had.

Ed looked over at Marcia. Naw. She wasn't alluring enough. She didn't know any tricks to take tricks. She was just a female.

An interesting one.

Not really. She wasn't chatty. She just looked around. She hadn't paid her half of the dinner bill nor had she returned his loan for her gambling spree.

He'd never considered she'd repay his stake. He'd invited her to go with him. Staking her was part of the date. She'd fed him supper. He'd taken her out for dessert.

They were already at the apartment house. He pulled up to the entrance and got out. She opened her own door and was out before he could help her.

She said, "It was a lovely evening. Thank you."

"I'll see you to your door."

"No need. I'll be okay."

"My father told me that I'd have to do this until I was married."

She questioned, "Did that keep you from marrying? You have a door fetish?"

He sighed with some patient drama. "You owe me a kiss."

She had the gall to inquire, "Why?"

"I've been a good host, I've spent the entire evening entertaining you and I have a tension headache."

She dug into her rather bulky purse. "I have an aspirin here somewhere. We'll fix that headache right now."

He expanded the premise. "A kiss does it. I can't take aspirin. I have to be kissed by a nubile woman. Preferably a nubile virgin."

She looked at him with interest. "Does that sort of baloney work for you?"

"With tenderhearted women, it does. Are you tenderhearted?"

"No." She came up with a small bottle. She set the bulky purse on the sidewalk by her foot and opened the aspirin bottle.

With a serious face, he said, "Aspirin doesn't do it for me."

"Oh." She observed him. There was a ghost of a smile that had touched her lips. Was it a smile or the beginnings of a sneer? A woman that age shouldn't be that smart.

She asked, "So. What do you do for a headache." It really wasn't a question. She was just curious what he'd say.

"Baseball. Tomorrow the Chiefs play. Go with me to the game and my headache will be cured."

She considered him quite seriously. "I'll have to see if I can arrange the time."

"I'll help you paint." My God, the ultimate sacrifice!

"No."

She'd said it so quickly that he frowned at her.

She amended, "I'll see if I can get my day's painting in earlier. I'll have to let you know. I'll leave a message on your phone by noon. Would that be too late?"

"I'll come over."

"No." It was quickly said.

Ed was caught by that. "Why not?"

"It's my obligation. I'll call you by noon."

He frowned. "That won't give us much time."

"I'll sing the 'Star-Spangled Banner' to you on the way—if I can manage to go."

By then, they were at her interim apartment. She had her keys out as her dad had obviously taught her.

She unlocked the door, and he stood watching her. Why had he invited her to the ball game? What idiot thing had made his mouth blurt out the invitation?

She had accepted.

She opened the door and turned. "It was a lovely evening. I haven't been so lavishly entertained in all my life. It was elegant. And so are you."

Then she stretched up along his body and kissed him!

Before he realized he hadn't been hit on the back of his head by a four-by-four, he was still only beginning to move his hands up—and she closed the door.

That quick!

He was still reeling from her kiss. How'd a twenty-three-year-old ever learn to do *that?*

In something of a paralyzed shock, he turned slowly and got to find out that going downstairs takes more concentration than he'd ever realized. Either that, or someone had rearranged the stairs.

He got into his car and drove around for a while. Since he'd lived in Peoria all his life, he didn't get lost. He finally found his way back to the compound. Then he walked around rather aimlessly.

He realized he was on the street below her Interim window. He felt the urge to yowl like a tomcat. She'd probably heave down one of her paint-splattered boots.

He walked back toward the compound a changed man. Changed? Entrapped? Of course not. It had just been a while since he'd been kissed that way. How rude of her not to carry a warning sign.

How embarrassing to be sundered by a neophyte's kiss. At his age? She was fourteen years younger than he! What in hell were the kids of today coming to?

On the sloppily plotted way back to the compound, Ed decided it wasn't her skill that had boggled him so shockingly. It was his almost six month acrid desert of being out of a job and being only friendly with uninterested women.

Ed hadn't had a kiss like that in too long. He was vulnerable. Well, they'd be at the ball game, so he ought to be relatively safe tomorrow.

At his place, he stripped, took a cold shower, two aspirin and drank a cup of warm milk. All night long, he slept the sleep of the gods who don't need sleep, and he chased young females in wisps of gossamer through sheep pastures.

Ed wakened with dark circles under his eyes and a disgruntled attitude. He was thirty-seven years old and past all this nonsense. After the ball game, he'd mark the new woman off his list.

List? What list?

Of course, he went to the apartment building to look around. Everything was being taken care of on schedule. The carpenters for the seriously needed repair work were courteous but went on working. No one had time for him. He went to his parents' house and sat talking to his dad at the kitchen table.

His dad asked, ''Who is she?''

Ed looked up in shock. "Who is who?"

His mother corrected, "Whom."

"What're'ya talking about?"

His mother said, "Don't slur your words to-gether."

His dad laughed.

That irritated the liver out of Ed. He soon excused himself, kissed his mother's cheek, patted his dad's shoulder... and left.

It was almost noon. He hurried home and punched his answering machine. Charlie had called. He sounded better. They were having a supper party on Friday. Bring a French loaf.

Carl had called to say hello. Call back.

John from California called, "You can see the state is stable. Come see us."

And the neophyte had called to say, "It's a go! See you at noon. I've been singing scales all night and will be able to do justice to the national anthem."

Sassy. This was the last time he'd see her. It was just a good thing he was rejecting her.

How interesting it was that she was getting easier with him just as he was freezing up. Hmmmm.

Marcia was at the outside door dressed in a long-sleeved cotton shirt, long cotton trousers, a billed hat and walking sports shoes. She had an over-the-shoulder looped carryall.

She didn't wait for him to get out and escort her to the car; he just had to reach over and unlock the door as she tugged at the door handle,

She grinned and said, "This is the perfect day."

How come she hadn't been this enthusiastic when he was considering her? He was rejecting her. This was the last time they'd be together. He could be pleasant.

She moved her bag carefully and explained, "I realize we'll eat hot dogs. You can't go to a baseball game and eat anything else and still be true to tradition."

He nodded soberly.

She laughed. "I brought lemonade. I figured during the afternoon you'd want a couple of beers. You can't drive under the influence, so I'll be sober and drive you home. You're only a mile from the apartments, so I can walk back. You are allowed, this time, to drink beer but not get soused."

"Soused?"

"You may indulge but not get drunk."

He briefly slid his eyes over to her. If he *seemed* to get drunk, she might be Samaritan enough to put him to bed— Yeah. He'd get her.

Such a decision can be tricky.

As Ed drove them along, she sang the "Star-Spangled Banner" quite well. She did it with respect, quite seriously, and wiped her eyes when she'd finished. She said, "It gets me every time."

He cleared his throat, but he didn't say anything. The words of the song got to him, too.

Both being from Peoria, in the baseball crowd they did see quite a few people they knew. That wasn't unusual for home folks. They saw family, those from work, from schools they'd attended and neighborhood friends.

While traditionally, the Hollingsworths sat along the first baseline, the Phillips kin were third base devotees. The ill-assorted pair sat along the first baseline. In their case, the identities were reversed. She was the big-eyed owl and he was a tomcat.

They called to people and they waved at others, and he found some people to sit among.

Marcia fit right in. She was younger than all of the women. And there were a good number of kids scattered throughout the bunch. Ed was especially aware of how many kids were there. They were the offspring of his friends.

Had he married when they had, he could have a pool of stretching out teenagers sitting with him. And Ed wondered what sort of father he'd have made.

That sounded as if he planned never to marry. Never to have kids. Maybe not. But the youth of the woman he was with was a clue to the lack of availability of an older woman.

Availability? Over there was Phyllis. She'd been divorced twice. There was Glenna. She'd had a couple of husbands. He could probably get someone his age who'd already experienced marriage and rejected it.

Did he *want* to be married? Probably not. If he'd wanted such a life, he could have had any number of women . . . along the time he was employed.

He looked at Marcia. She was too young for him. But he looked at the married men and the men who were no longer married but who had brought the kids along today, and he saw the interest in their eyes as they regarded Marcia.

Ed wouldn't tell any of those tomcats this was his last date with her because he was giving up on her. He could give her that much protection.

He noted how amused she was over a man's raucous hollering at the enemy team.

One really irritating thing about discarding a woman is that she can become so attractive in the time a man has chosen to part from her. Marcia was a real irritation. She was so funny and so charming and so involved in the game! She yelled at the opposing team. She'd make a good Cubs fan.

They had hot dogs almost right away, and Ed had a beer. Marcia took out her thermos from her shoulder bag sitting between her feet. She drank lemonade.

With all the hoopla, there was a lot of hilarity and chaffing. The game was going to the Chiefs and that made the crowd even more sassy.

And during all that time, Ed had sneakily collected beer cans from in back of them and along the way. When Marcia and a bunch of the kids went for more hot dogs, Ed had asked the guys in front of them to give him a couple of cans. Something different from what he already had.

Ed had an impressive collection just by the fifth inning. When he acted drunk, she'd be convinced.

The mid-seventh inning stretch allowed them to sing The Song and to stretch and wave at the cameras and laugh. It was as they sat down that Marcia noticed all the beer cans under Ed's feet. She was amazed!

She was also sobered. She didn't say anything to Ed, but she did look at him in order to judge his conduct.

By then he'd had two beers. But he didn't mention the gathering of the other empty cans. He smiled at her. He smiled a nearly closed eyes, happy smile. And his head wobbled just a tad.

Marcia told Ed, "I drive home."

With some careful skill, he took the car keys from his pocket and put them deliberately into her hand.

She said, "No more beer."

He nodded and his head wasn't entirely sure how far to go with it. He was so careful.

The game went into extra innings. The field lights came on as the dusk deepened. It was a switch leader game with both teams catching up to keep the score even.

And with the game over, the Chiefs' fans hollering in celebration, Marcia asked two unencumbered male friends of Ed's if they'd help her get Ed to the car.

They laughed and said, "Sure." And then they punched Ed's shoulder and slapped him on the back.

They weren't fooled for a minute. They'd donated a can or two to the pile under Ed's feet.

As the two very amused friends walked on either side of a slightly unsteady Ed to get through the pack of people, Ed said, "Sssuuupper," quite seriously. The "su" had apparently been a problem to get past.

The men jocularly offered to Marcia, "We'll go along with you and get him into bed for you."

Ed said, "I can do that for—my*self!*"

And the two slapped Ed on his shoulders and retorted, "I'll just bet you can."

As they finally got to the car, Marcia asked the two, "Can you get him into the front seat and buckle his belt? No. Maybe he ought to be in the back seat."

Ed objected.

The two helpers thought that was hilarious.

Marcia told Ed slowly and distinctly, "I can't have you wobbling around when I'm driving. And you might throw up. If you feel that way, here's my hat."

That hunched the two friends over with laughter. And they did, indeed, put Ed into the back seat. They buckled him into the seat belt and closed the door. Then they told Marcia, "We'll follow you."

Ed said, "No!" quite clearly.

Marcia told the laughing two, "Never mind. I can handle it now. Thank you."

"You sure?" They pushed.

She went to the driver's side, and across the top of the car, she promised them, "No problem."

She got into the driver's seat and buckled her belt, adjusting it to her lesser body.

Ordinarily Ed hated having his seat, mirror and seat belt fooled with by another person. That time, he didn't object. He sat quietly until she started the car. He said, "Sssuuupper."

Marcia replied, "Yes."

"Mc—Don-nalds."

"Right."

And he went to sleep. He snored quietly, a nice bubbly snore. She drove alone in the barely invaded silence. She skipped McDonald's and drove them to the compound.

Marcia had figured that Rudolf would be there if she couldn't move Ed. She drove between the cement posts that held the open gates. She parked in front of Ed's door.

He was home.

He sat feigning sleep.

She took the keys from the ignition. She exited, went around and opened the car door. Ed was very relaxed. She shook him a little and said, "Ed?"

He opened clear eyes and smiled at her.

She was surprised his eyes were so clear and that was the cause of her first suspicion. But she followed along with what was more than likely a farce. She told him, "We're at your place. Can you get out by yourself?"

He considered it carefully, then he said a slurring, "Sure."

Marcia stepped back.

He did a perfect imitation of a controlled drunk. He didn't stagger; he appeared to control his steps. It was brilliant. She had to admire it. She stood back and watched. She was no longer fooled. He was doing it all deliberately.

She thought: Why would he do that? Yeah. Maybe.

Her eyes narrowed slightly. "Can you make it into your place?"

His regard measured the distance to his door. "I can do it."

9

There is just something about a skilled man that is intriguing. Marcia was curious to see how Ed would conduct himself. That he was pretending to be carefully in control was now obvious. She should have been suspicious of the very number of empty beer cans. He'd overdone it.

But he *had* maintained a perfect facade of a practiced drunk. Instead of being sloppily out of control, he was carefully pretending to be a drunk who was in control of himself.

He was quite clever at it. That indicated that she was in danger. It was a challenge. She took his arm and led him to his door.

She asked, "Do you have the key?"

Slurring the words just a little, he replied, "It's in my pant pocket."

Mmm-hmmm. She considered him. He wanted her to fish around for a key that was probably in his hip pocket. She fooled him. She patted the pocket at the top of his leg. It held change.

She reached to pat the other pocket. He stumbled and caught her to him to steady himself.

They were face-to-face. He was looking into her eyes with a clear, steady look of evaluation. He was figuring out just how to go about seducing her.

Oddly, she broke his grasp with ease and no seeming effort. She patted the top of his other thigh and said, "This pocket."

With a quick dip, she brought out the house keys without touching against his body.

How'd she do that?

She'd put the key into the door and opened it. She said, "Good night."

He asked, "Is this my place?" He squinted and looked around.

She became amused. "Yes."

"Turn on the light."

She did hesitate. But then she went into his apartment and remembered where a lamp was. She turned it on, then looked to see where he was.

He was right behind her. How had he moved so quickly? Well, it was his place and he was only pretending to be incapacitated.

What would he do next? It was an interesting but not very difficult question. How would he make the approach?

His words slurred. "You're very nice."

She didn't laugh. She did smile a tad, but she didn't guffaw. She asked, "Can you get into bed by yourself? Or do you prefer the couch?"

"Which do you prefer?" He was soberly curious.

And she replied, "I have a fairly good bed at my place."

He looked around as if to assimilate where he actually was and asked in some disappointment, "Aren't we staying here?"

"You are. This is your place."

"Stay with me."

She chuckled in her throat. "No. Not when you don't know what you're doing."

"I would know."

"I'll bet you would."

"Help me."

With some irony, she inquired, "Are you too full of beer?"

And he regarded her quite seriously. "I'm not drunk."

She pretended to scoff. "Of course not."

"I had two beers the entire afternoon. I'm stone-cold sober."

She chewed on her lip to stop her laugh but her eyes danced and she said, "Yeah."

"I really am." His voice was gentle.

"I know." She reached up and mussed his hair as she started out his door. But she found herself plastered to him, and his mouth came down on hers with such a burning hunger.

She hadn't expected her body's reaction. She was shocked by the thrill that rampaged through her nervous system and whirled around intensely in a very private area.

But the worst part of it was that her brain was scrambled. She was gasping and making strange little hungry noises. She was!

How shockingly primitive.

Gutturally, he begged, "Love me."

She was incapable of replying. She became aware of that just as her voice said logically, "If I did, you wouldn't even remember we'd made love."

"I'd treasure the loving forever." He was leaving Peoria and soon. He couldn't pretend that he'd be there with her. He was limiting it to one encounter.

She caught that. He would "treasure" making love with her. This man who was a part-time rent collector. She wasn't put off. She'd been curious forever. Since Joe D had told her at eight that she'd like it.

Maybe now was the time. He was a sneaky man. That kind of man sneaked away after a time. He'd leave town.

His family was there.

"Love me. I ache for you. You're driving me crazy. I need you."

She scoffed, "You wouldn't pull a farce with me."

"I just wanted you to come home with me. I couldn't think of any other excuse but that I needed you. And, Marcia, I hurt for you."

"A long dry spell?"

"Don't be sassy. I've waited all this time for you to know me and see me as a good man. I've been careful. I don't have any of the diseases, and I have protection for you. Scouts' honor.''

"So you were a Boy Scout?"

"Dad kept us boys busy."

"That was nice."

Ed explained, "He'd managed to work in a bunch of kids. There are five of us."

"I don't want any children. I'm not the maternal type."

"I've told you I'll take good care of you."

"You say that now. How do I know what you're capable of doing?"

And he assured her, "I'm very careful and I've never had any complaints."

"If I lie down with you in your bed and allow you the liberty of my body, what do I get out of this?"

"You—charge?"

She went scarlet. "No!"

"You've been with other guys." That was the questioning statement, as if he'd said what was true and wasn't inquiring.

"I have brothers beside my dad. They are all big and very sure I have good care . . . and no hanky-panky."

With the skill of his age, he assured her, "I'd make love to you. I don't just fool around for my own satisfaction."

"How many women have you . . . had?"

"Two."

"How old were you?"

"Sixteen. She was twenty and it was her idea."

Marcia gasped, "You were—seduced?"

"I was shocked."

She grinned at him. "Didn't you fight her off?"

"She really took me by surprise. I thought it was just Show and Tell. But she was very...aggressive!"

Marcia laughed. It was a wonderful, soft sound. "Were you offended?"

"It was really something. With her, it was just right."

"She was wicked." Marcia was sure.

He shook his head in his long-ago amazement. "She was heaven, while it lasted."

"She found another...source?"

He put out a helpless hand and admitted, "Yeah. An old guy who was even older than she."

"How rude of her."

He nodded emphatically. "My thoughts exactly."

"So you're practiced. Are you...skilled?"

"I'm slow and careful. You'll love it. It's what you were made to do. You'll realize that right away."

"My mother doesn't think the way you do."

"She's a woman. Men understand such things. They're right. You need to let me show you what it's like..." He'd almost added, *while I'm still around to teach you!* He couldn't tell her he was leaving Peoria very soon. The information might cool her.

"So you're leaving Peoria?"

He was startled! Had he spoken aloud? Was he becoming senile at thirty-seven? His lips parted in shock.

"If you *are* leaving, I could sample you. And you wouldn't be around as a constant reminder that I'd let you."

He relaxed considerably. She was going to give in. He said, "As a matter of fact, I'm going to California."

"How soon?"

"As soon as I settle things up here."

She considered him. She reached up and rumpled his hair with one hand. Then she cocked her head sassily and told him, "Well, why not?"

She shocked him. He swallowed rather awkwardly and gasped. He did not choke, which was rather astonishing. He asked, "Now?"

She could hear the excited tremble in his voice. She said, "Why not?" Then she asked quickly, "You do have condoms?"

"Oh, yes."

"Are they a—recent purchase?"

"Why do you ask that?" He looked at her with some curiosity.

"If you're after me, it must be some time since you found a willing woman. That could be a while back."

"Why do you think I've had a long, dry spell?"

She shrugged marvelously and replied, "You're—after me." And she waited for what he would reply.

"I saw you in that empty room that Elinor had abandoned, and I figured at first you were just like her. Then when I got to know you, I wanted you for you and not for what you might be."

"You used—Elinor?"

"Oh, for Pete's sake, no!" And he looked indignant.

"Well, I am glad about that. We'll do it. How do we begin?"

"You kiss me."

She considered. "That sounds rather rash. Why don't you kiss me? I'll decide then."

"Do you mean you'd let me kiss you, a really serious kiss, and *then* you'll tell me if I can go on?"

"Yeah." She watched him with some interest.

"What about those guys that are helping you paint? You been with any of them?"

"Nope. You'll be my first."

"How'd you keep them away?" He frowned a little as he watched her.

"They aren't interested in me, at all."

"How do you know?"

"Believe me, they are married to women they like. They aren't interested in me in that way."

"They glare at me."

She licked her grin. "Does that scare you?"

"Not enough." His voice then clacked as he licked his own lips and told her seriously, "It's you that scares me. Kiss me. Kiss me like you want me."

"I suggested you kiss me first and let me decide if I want to, uh, let you."

He was earnest as he told her, "You will. You'll be all over me in your wild lust."

She laughed softly.

He cautioned her, "That kind of laugh gets a woman in a whole lot of trouble."

"Why?" Her smile stayed and she looked up at him in a very smug manner.

"Because it lights up a man."

"Electricity or coal oil?"

"Be careful." His tone chided her. "You have to know you're testing me."

"Why?"

"I'm still in control of myself. Don't flirt that way unless you mean it."

She laughed with such humor.

"How'd you learn to laugh that way?"

"What way?" But her eyes teased him.

"Are you seeing how far you can go with me? Or are you that naive?"

"Yeah."

"Which one?" His eyes were intense and his breathing was harsh.

"Both."

It was interesting to Marcia that he didn't tussle with her right away. Instead he took her carefully into his arms and against him. He was breathing audibly and the sound of it was harsh.

But the interesting thing was, he was giving her time to change her mind. Marcia figured he must be very practiced to do that so well.

She didn't push him away, so he kissed her. It was long, wet and very serious. His tongue touched her lips in a slow flick. It was sensual.

Her sex was intensely interested. Her own breathing was rather erratic as she kissed him back.

His body was so hard against hers. He was strong. His arms were just like the romance novels said. His really were bands of steel. And she'd always snorted over the idea of such a thing. The writers had been right.

Having read enough of the books, Marcia waited for him to press against her stomach. Slowly, gathering her closer, his kiss harder, he did that.

His sex was so hard that her brain was a little shocked. However, her body reacted in a scandalously salacious manner.

Her body chose to rub against him, and Ed groaned almost harshly. He lifted his mouth from her swollen one; and he looked at her as if he'd only just found her and was surprised.

He asked, "How many men have you ruined?"

"None . . . so far."

"I shudder to think what you'll do to me."

And she had the audacity to reply, "Yeah." But she smiled!

Then she closed her eyes and wiggled herself against him as she made throaty sounds. It was erotic.

It was for Ed, too. And he tried to get his brain cells together and organized but they responded to his command with, "Aw, what the hell! Go ahead!"

He was so peaked that he scooped her up just like one of the romances and he carried her effortlessly into his bedroom.

She looked around. "Not the rug in the living room?"

"This is better."

And she asked, "What's the difference?"

"Your back won't be abraded, and the bedsprings will help you bounce me."

"Why... bounce?"

"I'll explain as I go along."

"Do I take off my clothes?"

Hoarsely he said a very serious, "Yes." Then he added, "I'll help."

But he was quickly shedding his own clothing. She watched in some astonishment. Men wear more clothing than women. He apparently knew exactly what to take off first, and how to get rid of the rest. He did it very, very quickly.

He was naked.

While Marcia had seen naked pictures of men, she had never seen a real one without some sort of groin covering. Not a live one. She wasn't sure where to look. But she did.

Ed assured her, "It's friendly."

She observed seriously, "It turns up."

And he said very quickly, "It'll be okay."

"I didn't know they turned up."

He responded to any alarm. "It'll fit."

"How fascinating!" She then asked, "Is that why rhino's horns are cut off?"

"I don't know."

He was undressing her. He unbuttoned every little button on her shirt. His hands trembled.

She said, "I can do that faster."

"I'm showing that I have control and I'm not ripping the buttons off."

She looked up at his face. "Is that why you're so slow?"

He looked into her eyes. "You want this faster?"

"No."

He asked, "Do you want me?"

She didn't reply verbally, she just nodded quite seriously.

His breathing was erratic so he had to lick his lips and swallow rather loudly. He told her, "You're going to get me."

So she stood there. But she did notice his sex was eager. Then she put her hand on it to control it, and Ed gasped and panted.

"What's the matter?"

"Honey, I'm really triggered. I'm trying to control it. I'm reciting the multiplication tables."

"How far are you?"

"Pretty soon."

"In the multiplication tables," she clarified.

"Two times two."

"Four."

"Thank you. I was stymied."

She chuckled.

"That's a salacious chuckle."

"I think you're funny."

"What else do you think about me?"

"You need a better job."

"I'm considering one."

"Doing what?"

As he completed the buttons, he opened her shirt to look at her red lace bra. He mentioned vaguely, "Maybe we can discuss that later. I'd rather tell you how beautiful you are."

"Okay."

"You're a work of art," he mentioned distractedly as he solved her zipper on her trousers. He unbuttoned the button and unzipped her pants.

She observed, "You did your own pants. You didn't let me do your zipper."

"You need to learn how to run a man's zipper down and not neuter him."

"There's danger in that? From a zipper?"

"Yeah."

"You must be fragile."

"I am." His conscience didn't bother him at all. A woman had to know how vulnerable and fragile a man was.

But he squatted down and lifted first her one foot and then the other from her pant legs. He was very concentrated. Then he looked up her body.

She watched him as he observed her form. She knew she was average. But he squatted there and he looked on her as if she was a goddess. How clever of him.

He said, "Wow."

And she did reply, "This old thing?"

He rose so effortlessly. He had good coordination. And he stood before her.

She told him, "You're in good physical shape. Your coordination is very good."

He murmured, "Thank you."

She began an open gesture but he took her against him and he really, really kissed her. His hands moved her so that her naked breasts were rubbed against the hair on his chest. It was breathtakingly erotic.

She asked, "How'd you learn to do that?"

"What?" He was distracted.

"Rub me against you so I could feel your body hair. It was thrilling."

"I have all kinds, you can try any of it anytime."

"Why, thank y—"

He kissed her again.

Then he lifted her onto his arms and carried her around the room for a while.

Rather logically, she asked, "Why are you carrying me around?"

And he replied, "To calm me down a little."

"Are you excited?"

"I'm on overload."

She considered him and gave her opinion, "You act a little vague."

"I'm still doing the multiplication tables."

He'd seemed distracted, so that was the reason. "How far along do you have to go?"

That caught his attention. "Where?"

She gestured openly, and he got to watch her do that. She explained, "In the multiplication tables."

He nodded once in understanding and replied, "It all depends on how quickly you want to get this over. If you're the wham-bam-thank-you-ma'am type, we can get it over right now."

She shifted in his arms and wiggled a little getting comfortable, then she smiled nicely and asked, "Where did you go to school?"

He had to sit down, he laughed so hard. She was on his lap and her legs were over the arm of the chair, so he pulled his arm from under her knees and he used his hand to explore her body.

"Are you supposed to do that?"

Concentrated, he replied, "If you don't like it, tell me."

"I like it, but it seems to be quite bold of you."

"I'll let you do the same to me." And true to his word, he lay back and left his upper body open for her examination. His sex was not behaving quite so well. It was banging against her bottom.

She whispered, "It's alive."

He nodded. "I had noticed. It wants you."

"To do what?" She completed his sentence.

"To be comforted and soothed. It's just about crazy to get inside you."

"Where're the condoms? It needs one."

He groaned.

She put her hand to the side of his face in empathy and told him, "I'll put it on for you."

He laughed.

"Now, why was that funny?"

"Honey, you start fooling around trying to get a condom on Jake there, and it'll all be over—"

"Jake?" She frowned and looked around. "I just want to put the condom on you."

"Some guys name their sexes. You'll hear about Osgood, or Pete, or Goodwill or my Jake. He's a friend who lives on me and shares."

She grinned but she shook her head with her tolerance.

In a roughened, low voice he said, "You could kiss me."

So she reached up and kissed his mouth. He made savoring sounds and his hand curled around her here and there. He groaned and breathed as he kneaded her.

But he had begun to catch her attention, and her own body was getting tense and excited. She said, "Ed..."

"Want me?"

"You know, I think I do."

He smiled as his hands moved, giving her excitements and thrills. He kissed her and his hands worked her. She began to moan and to sigh. She lay back with her head on his shoulder.

Her body was vulnerable to his curiosity and she allowed it. She murmured and her eyes closed and her lips were reddened. She moved in twitches and was lax and sinuous, but he was as hard as iron.

His breathing was harsh as she moved her hand on him. He didn't let her roll on the condom. "If you did that, you'd have to sit around, reading some *Field and Stream* magazines until I was ready again...Jake and me."

"When?"

"You're sassy. When do you want me?"

"I'd like to try it . . . now."

"Yeah. I just hope I can last long enough."

"Long . . . enough? For what?"

"For you." He leaned to kiss her nose and he fondled her, smoothing his hands along her. He told her, "You're beautiful."

"Actually, I'm just like any woman."

"No. You're special. You're you." Then he looked into her eyes, and she saw something like surprise in his.

He shivered to find he cared for her unduly. It was the only thing that could have distracted him enough to really make love with her.

But he lifted her as he stood up from the chair. Being able to do that was quite astonishing to him. He carried her to the bed with some emotion.

And when he laid her down so that her head was on his pillow, he looked at her differently. It was scary. . . for *him*. He'd never felt that way about any woman.

Ed eased down beside her and took her into his arms to hold her close to him. And his body knew hers. They made exquisite love. His strange attitude toward her caused his slowness, and she was one of the few women who climaxed on the first try.

It was stupendous and it was their first try. How amazing!

There was a little blood on the sheet, which caused his heart to squeeze in emotion. She didn't even notice. She lay with her eyes closed and a slight smug smile on her swollen lips.

He held her hand. They were silent.

Her lips moved and she asked Ed, "How soon can we do it again?"

He put his forearm dramatically across his eyes and groaned.

After a while, they showered together. And they were slow about washing their bodies. He mentioned that she might want to go back to her apartment—or she could decide to stay there with him. The bed was big enough.

He expected her to gasp at the time, but she just stretched and smiled. "I believe I could become addicted."

"It's because you waited for me before you did it."

How like a man to say something so earnestly.

She kissed him sweetly but she said, "I really have to get back to the apartment."

He argued quite brilliantly in opposition, but she won.

How strange it was for him to let go of her. He was reluctant to take her to his car.

As they drove along, she was watching around, turning her head to see farther. She only glanced at him. But she did smile slightly.

10

As Ed drove Marcia up to the door of the apartment building, the headlights beamed across two men who were standing near the entrance. While it was late, they looked harmless to Ed. They were standing easy and watching the car with lazy noninterest.

"Ah-h-h!" Marcia's voice was soft. "As soon as I get out, you take off."

Ed became indignant. Just why should *he* take off? She wasn't meeting those guys. It was really rather late. Why were they there watching cars? Who were they? Ed was intense and indignant.

Marcia said it again, "Get out of here." She was already leaving the car.

So Ed turned off the ignition, took the keys from the car, got out on his side and walked stiff-legged around the hood of the car. He was a bit territorial.

The two men watched the couple and they didn't move at all. No threat.

Through her teeth, Marcia told Ed, "Get out of here!"

There was a slight move by one of the men to turn away.

Marcia thrust her hand into her purse and came up with a really nasty looking gun!

Just that quick, she was saying, "Police! Freeze!"

That overrode Ed's, "I'm allergic to guns in—"

The other guy said, "Hey! I'm legit! Don't point that nasty thing at me! My friend'll get edgy."

Marcia said forcefully and very positively, "Get over there, both of you. Get your feet spread, put your hands on the wall and don't move otherwise."

The other guy slouched a little and laughed with a male chuckle of tolerance.

In an utterly deadly voice that was worse than a mother's stern warning, Marcia said quietly, "Do it." Then she spoke into something that came out of her shoulder-slung, loaded purse. A radio?

Ed felt really ticked with her trying to act like a cop. What was her purpose? He opened his mouth... and a squad car came up in only a rush of quiet sound. The passenger cop was out of the car in a flick of time and his gun was on the two.

Who ever heard of a police response that happened that fast? Ed was stunned.

The accosted two took the male cop more seriously, especially because the driver of the squad car had come out of the driver's seat and also had a gun.

The two slouchers did what they were told to do and did it quickly. The cops asked Marcia, "Him?" They indicated Ed.

She replied, "No."

One cop scoffed at her response, declaring, "He looks sneaky to me."

She was patient.

The other asked, "Want us to check him out?"

She was kind. "No."

The two against the brick wall protested the entire time.

"We didn't even do nothing! We was just walking along, and she got all upset! You need to take her to a shrink."

The male cop said, "We've been looking for you."

"For us?" They were astonished.

"Yeah. Chicago contacted us not two days ago. Come along. We reserved our best suite for you guys."

"Wait a minute! We just got here! We ain't done nothing!"

"Chicago's missed you guys. They felt real grief when you left. They've been looking everywhere. They want to see you again . . . as soon as possible."

And amazingly in no time at all, the two from Chicago were getting a free ride to the clink. That left the couple there, alone.

It seemed very quiet.

Ed looked at his recent lover and inquired, "You're a . . . cop?"

"Mmm-hmmm."

"Where's your badge?"

She took it from her purse.

He examined it minutely. Grudgingly he admitted, "It looks legit."

"It is."

"What are you doing painting apartments?"

"Cops aren't paid enough."

"Everybody says that."

So she said, "How about I have a secret yearning for you?"

He looked at her with great impatient impatience. He said it again, "A cop." He said it sourly.

And she shrugged. "Yeah."

"You don't act like a cop... well, you haven't until right now. Why didn't you tell me? You coulda gotten me killed, here, trying to protect you."

"I told you to get going. Twice."

"How'd you know what they'd do? You couldn't'a handled them both. You're just lucky I was along."

She solemnly bit into her lower lip and didn't say anything.

"You've rattled me. How can I trust you to stay here by yourself if everybody knows you're a cop?"

"The Revenge Of the Earth People?"

"Something like that."

"Most people don't mind about cops. There are even people who like us."

"Who?"

She grinned at him "You, for one."

"I didn't know the real you." He was disgruntled. He watched her sourly. "That cop at the river gambling place, is he a guy you know?"

"We're not kin, but he told my dad that you look like a sloucher."

"A sloucher!" He straightened up, offended.

She explained kindly, "A guy that'll slouch out on a woman."

Well, that was true. Since it was, he became indignant. He had no other choice. He said, "I'll tell my parents you reported this to me."

She considered him and then advised, "If you do it well enough, with enough indignation, we could start a good family feud."

"I'm leaving." It was blurted out before he could stop it. He bit into his tongue and watched what her reaction would be.

She smiled. "Good night. I'd kiss you but I've given you your share for this week."

He regarded her gloomily. He probably wouldn't be around for next week's donation of her kisses. He said a sour, "Good night." Then he caught himself. "I'll see you upstairs . . . to your place."

As they went into the building, he asked her, "If you're a cop, you have to know Elinor is a deadbeat."

"Yeah."

"Then why did you move into her place?"

"I knew it was empty."

That was logical. "Why didn't you rent it? Why did you just . . . move in?"

She turned an honest face to his and replied, "She said she'd paid two months in advance."

He gave her an excessively disbelieving look of disgust.

Marcia shrugged. "It sounded okay to me."

"You're as bad as she is."

She was sassy. "No. I've just proven I'm—badder."

He melted. "Oh, Marcia, you aren't bad. You're compassionate and kind."

With it so late and silent in the building, she clamped one hand over her mouth to try to stop the spurt of hilarity.

Ed watched her youthful sassiness and was irritated. She was too young for him. He put his hands into his pants pockets and glanced over at her as they went up another flight of stairs.

She was silent. But he noticed that she still was looking around. She wasn't naturally that way. She did it because the police had trained her to know where she was and who else was there.

Ed wondered who else she was looking for besides those two guys from Chicago? And he found it distasteful that she could apprehend two big guys he'd hesitate approaching.

She'd been so calm, so positive. She'd been professional.

It was just as well he was going to California.

At her door he observed her put her key in the lock. He said, "I get a good-night kiss."

She grinned. "You already had that kind. You've used up the whole supply."

"I get a kiss."

She looked in her purse and felt her pockets as—

He kissed her. It was a full-out passionate, brain-ruining one. He did it deliberately.

She became a malleable mass. He was jittery. He didn't mind because it satisfied him to see her wobbled.

Now, why would such a thing satisfy him?

She'd confronted two dangerous men all by herself and was successful. She'd outshone him. He was... jealous. He wouldn't have known what to do or how to handle those guys.

Well, she'd had a gun.

But she'd known exactly how to use it. And he didn't.

She couldn't turn the knob on her door. He did that for her. She nodded and stumbled into her apartment. She closed the door gently as she murmured something or the other. And Ed was alone in the hall.

He was filled with superiority. He'd wobbled her.

It was only then that he understood why she lugged around that big shoulder bag purse.

He went down the two flights of stairs and walked almost all the way to the compound before he remembered his car was back at her apartment house.

It was hers?

It was where she lived.

She wasn't paying rent.

Well. She *was* painting. She was a little slow, but she was almost paying her rent.

On two apartments.

So? Well. He'd figure it out!

He went back for his car and drove it back to the compound. He was tired enough to sleep. And he did sleep. But again, he dreamed.

Wow. Did he ever dream! Any ordinary man would have slept the sleep of a surfeit body. Not him. *He* had to spend all that restless time . . . dreaming.

It was a lot like being fourteen again.

Who the hell wants to be fourteen?

Well, a fourteen-year-old thinks it's grown up. Ed was twenty-three years older. He could have fathered a kid who was now fourteen. That was sobering.

Ed turned in bed and plumped up the pillow. He smoothed it and laid the side of his head on it. He was curled up and wide awake.

She came back inside his head. What other "she" was there? And it was only then that he understood his restless night. Her fragrance was on the pillow. No wonder.

The whole episode was probably because he was going to leave Peoria. In long generations, he'd be the first of his family to absence himself from his hometown. His mother would be stunned, and his father would leak tears.

That very attitude was what had kept their sons in Peoria. Ed would leave. The very thought depressed him.

He got out of bed and it was too early to be up. It was too early to even be awake. The morning paper wasn't even there.

Ed walked over to the front window in the living room to look out across the compound to the river. It was raining. The day was as gloomy as he. How appropriate.

He was going to California. He would go. And he wondered if Marcia would like to go along—just for the ride—and help him get settled.

The phone rang right on schedule. It would be Marcia just awake and stretching. She'd want to hear his voice and what he'd say... after last night.

He picked up the phone and said in his bedroom voice, "This is Ed Hollingsworth." The office habit of response had clung to his subconscious.

"Hello, Ed. Sorry to be so early but I've had a hard time getting you. My name's Billy Joe Mueller. I'm calling from TEXAS. Ever hear of the place?"

"A hint of it, now and again."

"Good. We do hate to surprise people. We're a computer company?" The questioning statement. "We invent things. We need a good office manager." Billy Joe was confident and quoted a whopping salary and benefits that would have boggled an alert man.

Billy Joe went on to say, "A friend of yours named Charlie Jones talked with us last week and gave us your credentials. They are attention-getting."

"Thank you."

"We'd like a look at the package. Our treat, we'd like you to come on down here and let us show you around this glorious land. How about it?"

"Well, when?"

"You can get a plane out today at—"

Ed laughed. "Give me a couple of days. I have to have my suit cleaned." A man in Ed's position didn't fool anyone.

And Billy Joe scoffed. "Come in jeans. We're casual. Actually, we're a little tacky. It soothes Yankees."

They arranged the time, said their farewells and Ed slowly hung up. Then he called Charlie.

Charlie answered as usual, "Yo."

"What do you know about this conglomerate down near Dallas?"

"Ah." Charlie was satisfied. "So they did call you."

"How'd you work this?"

"They've hired me. I suggested you. I'd miss your ugly face, and this solved that. I need a bro' down th—yonder."

Ed commented thoughtfully, "You're getting into the language well."

Charlie agreed. "It's catching."

Ed scoffed, "Bought your boots yet?"

And Charlie replied readily, "I'm being fitted for them. They've taken a cast of my feet. And I've chosen the various kinds of leather."

"I can't believe this."

"Wait'll you see your office—down yonder."

Ed chided, "How'd you change language so fast?"

In a verbal shrug, Charlie replied, "It just...flows. You wait. You'll be talking right along with them."

"I've got that dangled carrot out in California."

"Decline." Charlie was sure. "Nothing's gonna touch the deal you'll get in TEXAS."

"Even *you* say the state in caps?"

Charlie was gentle. "When you've been there, you'll understand."

Ed observed thoughtfully, "So you're going to Texas."

"I can already tell—and over the phone, mind you—that you're not saying TEXAS right. Practice. I'll be in touch."

And Charlie hung up.

For a strange while, Ed just stared out of the window at the soft rain. Could he actually leave Peoria? He knew that Tex-TEXAS was different.

Ed felt a little strange. Tilted. Who would have believed something like this could come up, and *Charlie* had been the trigger!

Ed almost dialed Marcia's numbers...she had phones. One in both of her apartments. Instead, he went in and had a glass of orange juice and some instant decaf coffee. He was cutting down.

He looked through the whole place for a forgotten cigarette. He hadn't actually been aware that he was looking for one, therefore he finally stopped and sorted it out. He hadn't smoked in four years!

What was rattling him now?

It was that woman who was a—cop. Even as he thought the dismissive word, his face softened and his eyes became vacant.

He put on a clean jogging suit and ran through the rain over to the apartment house. He went inside and up the stairs. She didn't answer either knock.

If she wasn't there, where was she? Out on the streets of Peoria, trying to wrestle some mug into a police car? Ed became agitated. Neither door opened to his master key. All was silent.

As he reached the top of the stairs, Marcia came from the closer empty apartment and called softly to him.

Ed walked back toward her. "You didn't answer my knock."

"I was in the bathroom."

He gave a brilliant response. He said, "Oh." Then he added, "Are you okay?"

She blushed scarlet. She didn't reply. She just stood there, smiling.

His slow feet had gotten his body to hers, and he took her into his rain-wet arms and pressed her against his sopping body. He kissed her until neither of them could breathe correctly.

What was he doing? He slowly released her and just looked at her.

Marcia said, "I owe you for the jackpot."

Since she offered, he said, "No, the evening was my treat. I didn't win the jackpot, you did. It's yours."

Did she insist on paying him? No. She just grinned and said, "It was such a nice evening—"

"Winning money helps."

She ignored him and finished her sentence, "But last night was better."

She knew the right buttons to punch. He was melted caramel—sweet, soft and malleable—just like that.

He asked, "Anybody with you?" And he looked beyond her to her apartments.

"My brother is helping me paint."

"Oh."

Her eyes sparkled. "What did you have in mind to look so deflated?"

He regarded her for just a minute before his smile began.

She watched the smile grow as she grinned and licked her lips.

He looked beyond her and back down the stairs. No one was around, so he kissed her again.

It was a stupid thing to do, but he didn't realize it, then.

She fit against him so nicely. She was so soft. She wiggled a little to get closer and aroused him unduly.

He panted.

She drew back a little and put her hand to his cheek. "What's the matter?"

He regarded her soberly and told her the truth. "You really trigger me. I want you."

She grinned widely and replied, "Good."

"What's good about it?"

"I want to do it again. It was just so nice."

Earnestly, he urged, "Do it again, with me."

Sassily, she told him, "No one else offered."

And he was shocked. Could she have become twenty-three and not yet realized...? And he pitied all the guys who'd tried and hadn't been understood by her. But he was glad that had happened. And he was glad it had been nice for her. He asked, "What do you think about TEXAS?"

She considered the premise. Then she inquired kindly, "It's south of here? South and somewhat west?"

"Would you like to drive down with me to see it?"

"Are you going to Texas?"

"I've learned that one says TEXAS as if it's all in caps."

"Why is that?"

Ed shrugged. "It's the biggest state?"

"No, Alaska is."

Ed nodded. "Then it's probably a throwback to the time before Alaska was gobbled up. I'm going down there. Come along with me. It'll open up new horizons."

She whispered, "That was done last night."

He groaned as if with great pain.

"What's the matter?" She put her hand on his chest and looked up at him in concern.

"I want you, right now."

She grinned and shook her head, but she blushed scarlet.

So he kissed her.

When he finally lifted his mouth, he urged, "Come with me."

"I can't. Not right now. I'll come down to see you when I'm free."

"You *are* married?"

"No, silly. I'm working on . . . a project."

He asked tersely, "With the cops?"

"It's a survey. It should be over soon." She nodded with her words. "I can come down later. I would like to."

She shivered his insides. He coughed to clear his throat. "I'll be driving down on Friday morning. If you change your mind, you can go with me, then."

She considered it and said, "That does give me some elbow room. I'll let you know."

"Now?"

"No, silly. When I'm free."

"I'll be in touch. I'll call you. I'll see to it that you have my number and where I'll be."

"All right."

He carefully crowded her. She allowed him to again draw her very close as he hugged her to his wet body. He wasn't even aware of being so rain-soaked. He was hot. So was his wet jogging suit.

That amused her. Oh, well, she could change easily enough.

She looked around to see if anyone was observing them.

So Ed looked, too. He'd forgotten about looking for someone else. He kissed her.

It was the skyrocket type of kiss, and they left this planet.

Oddly, they heard voices. He made soothing sounds to her, but some yahoo took hold of Marcia's arm and said to Ed, "Let go! It's *now!*" And he slammed a gun belt into her hands.

Marcia exclaimed, "Oh! Now?"

And the lump confirmed it. "They just got here. It's *now!*"

Marcia wiggled and pushed Ed from her. "I've got to go."

Ed saw the big man was running down the stairs. He asked, "What—?"

"They're robbing the bank."

"Who?"

Another big man in coveralls came from the apartment and said, "Right now!"

And Marcia followed the guy recklessly down the stairs!

They were all *cops!*

Ed was offended. Then he went to the apartment to look out, and he saw the binoculars on the table in plain sight. It had been a stakeout. *That's* why she'd been there. She really wasn't a painter.

Ed picked up the binoculars and went to the window. He focused on her as she ran across the street to where some squad car had drawn up.

She was in danger!

Ed put the binoculars down and went out of the apartment, down the hall and down the stairs two at a time without any thought at all.

He ran all the way down the block and was stopped dead by a cop who asked for—ID.

Ed told the cop, "Marcia's over there."

"Yeah. Let's see your driver's license."

"I'm jogging. I've got to help her."

"She can take care of herself. Let me see some ID or you're going downtown."

The cop was serious.

Of course, being in jogging clothes, Ed carried no ID. He put out his arms and said again, "I've been jogging."

"Good for you. Go away. You're distracting me. It's just a good thing for you that I know who the hell you are. Now, shut up and stand aside."

Ed did that. He stretched and looked and moved and was snarled at by the nasty cop.

There was bedlam on beyond and—a gunshot!

The cop caught Ed as he ran past and slammed him against the side of a cruiser. The cop snarled, "Stay there! One move and I zap you."

It was only then that Ed realized the cop was almost as wired as he was.

Ed stood still. But he shivered with his need to find Marcia.

Was she all right? Where was she? His teeth rattled a little.

Ed took an arguing breath, and the cop didn't even turn around. He just growled and said real low and mean as he concentrated at a distance, "Shut up and stay still."

It was all over in only one . . . millennium. Ed was frayed. The cop wasn't much better. Other people came into sight. There she was! She was on her feet and directing people. She had a whistle in her mouth and she was getting people out of the way. She didn't need him. She was a pro.

Ed stood and just watched her. She was okay. She had to quit the force. Women had no business—at all—being cops. She could get hurt. She could have been . . . killed.

He stood a long while. She went to a squad car and left. The cop near Ed was directing traffic. People were rubbernecking and asking questions.

It was over.

She was all right.

Ed slowly went back to his compound. He could barely walk it. Instead of being jumpy, he was drained. He stood in the shower for a long time. He slowly came to the acknowledgment that he was lucky he was leaving Peoria.

If the job in TEXAS didn't work out, he'd go on to California.

It was a serious thing he was escaping there. Marcia was dangerous to a man who had survived women for thirty-seven years.

He could barely move. He found he wanted to cry. She'd been right in the middle of danger, and he'd been kept away from helping her. What all *else* would she get into?

It really was a good thing that he was leaving.

The car came into the compound with just a whisper. He glanced out of the window and saw her get out of the squad car. She came up to the door as he opened it.

She was full of herself. She was excited and laughing and gesturing, and he stood there assuring himself that she wasn't a ghost. She was real.

He heard her say, " . . . was easy! We did it!"

Ed replied, "You have to quit your job."

She stood still as her face sobered. She looked at him as an adult does to a recalcitrant child. She said,

"Why." It was not a question. It was an invitation for an adult to hear what the imbecile had as a reason for such a stupid remark.

"I can't stand it."

She frowned slightly. "You can't stand . . . what?"

"Not being able to help you."

That melted her down. It was she who was caramel all sweet and easy. She laughed so gently, deep in her throat. She went to Ed and put her arms around him.

But his arms were tense and crushing as he held her to him. "I can't handle you being a cop."

"Prejudice is not couth."

"Then I'm—uncouth."

"I hadn't noticed!" she exclaimed in some elaboration, but she laughed low in her throat. "Want to lie down a while and rest? I'd like to twiddle with you."

Ed scowled. "Playing cops turns you on?"

Marcia considered. "I don't think that's it. But I have been exuberant. We got them! Hah!"

"Who?"

"The bank robbers! They weren't smart enough to quit after the first one. Now they're really in trouble."

She walked away from Ed to the window. "Your neighbors will question you about the squad car being parked in front of your place."

"What should I tell them?"

She shrugged sassily. "Oh . . . that we finally caught up with you?"

He pushed. "Are you quitting your job?"

"No, but I have some time off. I can go with you, now. If you'd still like company down to Texas... whoops, sorry. TEXAS."

"Can you be ready by Friday?"

She grinned at Ed. "Yeah."

"You're supposed to say, 'Yes, sir.'"

"Oh."

"Aren't you gonna say it right?"

"No, sir."

He smiled slowly. Then he went to her and held her against him.

She said, "I can read a road map."

"That would help."

She was sly as she grinned wickedly. "You could fiddle around with my body."

And Ed hugged her tightly as he said in a foggy voice, "Done."

"Not yet."

There's nothing worse than a sassy woman. It was just a good thing he knew how to handle her.

* * * * *

FORTUNE'S Children™

New York Times Bestselling Author
REBECCA
BRANDEWYNE

Launches a new twelve-book series—FORTUNE'S CHILDREN
beginning in July 1996 with Book One

Hired Husband

Caroline Fortune knew her marriage to Nick Valkov was in
name only. She would help save the family business, Nick
would get a green card, and a paper marriage would suit both
of them. Until Caroline could no longer deny the feelings Nick
stirred in her and the practical union turned passionate.

MEET THE FORTUNES—a family whose legacy is greater than
riches. Because where there's a will...there's a wedding!

Look for Book Two, *The Millionaire and the Cowgirl*,
by Lisa Jackson. Available in August 1996 wherever Silhouette
books are sold.

This exciting new cross-line continuity series unites
five of your favorite authors as they weave five
connected novels about love, marriage—and
Daddy's unexpected need for a baby carriage!

Get ready for

THE BABY NOTION by Dixie Browning (SD#1011, 7/96)
Single gal Priscilla Barrington would do anything for a
baby—even visit the local sperm bank. Until cowboy
Jake Spencer set out to convince her to have a family
the natural—and much more exciting—way!

And the romance in New Hope, Texas, continues with:

BABY IN A BASKET
by Helen R. Myers (SR#1169, 8/96)

MARRIED...WITH TWINS!
by Jennifer Mikels (SSE#1054, 9/96)

HOW TO HOOK A HUSBAND (AND A BABY)
by Carolyn Zane (YT#29, 10/96)

DISCOVERED: DADDY
by Marilyn Pappano (IM#746, 11/96)

DADDY KNOWS LAST arrives in July...only from

DKL-D

Silhouette's recipe for a sizzling summer:

* Take the best-looking cowboy in South Dakota
* Mix in a brilliant bachelor
* Add a sexy, mysterious sheikh
* Combine their stories into one collection and you've got one sensational super-hot read!

Summer Sizzlers

MEN OF Summer

Three short stories by these favorite authors:

Kathleen Eagle
Joan Hohl
Barbara Faith

Available this July wherever Silhouette books are sold.

Look us up on-line at: http://www.romance.net

Silhouette®

SS96

Also available by popular author

LASS SMALL

Silhouette Desire®

#05755	BEWARE OF WIDOWS	$2.89	☐
#05817	*TWEED	$2.99	☐
#05830	A NEW YEAR	$2.99	☐
#05848	I'M GONNA GET YOU	$2.99	☐
#05860	SALTY AND FELICIA	$2.99 U.S.	☐
		$3.50 CAN.	☐
#05895	AN OBSOLETE MAN	$2.99 U.S.	☐
		$3.50 CAN.	☐

*Man of the Month

Yours Truly™

#52004	NOT LOOKING FOR A TEXAS MAN	$3.50 U.S.	☐
		$3.99 CAN.	☐

(limited quantities available on certain titles)

TOTAL AMOUNT	$
POSTAGE & HANDLING	$
($1.00 for one book, 50¢ for each additional)	
APPLICABLE TAXES**	$_____
TOTAL PAYABLE	$_____
(check or money order—please do not send cash)	

To order, complete this form and send it, along with a check or money order for the total above, payable to Silhouette Books, to: **In the U.S.**: 3010 Walden Avenue, P.O. Box 9077, Buffalo, NY 14269-9077; **In Canada**: P.O. Box 636, Fort Erie, Ontario, L2A 5X3.

Name: _____

Address: _____ City: _____

State/Prov. _____ Zip/Postal Code. _____

**New York residents remit applicable sales taxes.
  Canadian residents remit applicable GST and provincial taxes.   SLSBACK7

🔷 Silhouette®